W9-CFO-137

ROBAK'S CROSS

By Joe L. Hensley

ROBAK'S CROSS

JOE L. HENSLEY

PUBLISHED FOR THE CRIME CLUB BY
DOUBLEDAY & COMPANY, INC.
GARDEN CITY, NEW YORK
1985

All of the characters in this book
are fictitious, and any resemblance
to actual persons, living or dead,
is purely coincidental.

Library of Congress Cataloging in Publication Data

Hensley, Joe L., 1926–
  Robak's cross.

  I. Title.
PS3558.E55R6   1985   813'.54
ISBN 0-385-19995-3

Library of Congress Catalog Card Number 85–5234

This one's for Char, Guy, Jon, John, Ted, and Virginia, readers all.

ROBAK'S CROSS

CHAPTER ONE

Ann. Statutes: The state may seek a death sentence for murder by alleging, on a page separate from the rest of the charge, the existence of at least one of the aggravating circumstances listed in subsection a.

(a6) The defendant committed the crime by lying in wait.

"You have the jury again, Mr. Robak," Judge Harner said. He looked tired.

I nodded and quit watching the tribe of squirrels playing summer games in the trees outside the courtroom windows. In my next life my plans are to be either a squirrel or a golf pro. I knew I was part of the reason the judge was tired. I'd been hard at *voir dire* for almost four days in Bington's decaying courtroom with Herman Leaks, the county prosecutor. We'd asked prospective jurors questions worth asking and some that weren't. Herman brings out the *voir dire* worst in me because he's a circular, never-ending bastard. He's detestable enough that I tend to become detestable myself when I engage in courtroom combat with him. We hate each other.

Together we'd run helter-skelter through a venire of two hundred and Judge Harner was getting very four-day snappish with both of us. Now, sitting huddled in the back of the courtroom, perhaps hoping they'd be ignored, were about a score of possible jurors. It was late Friday afternoon. I'd used my final peremptory challenge in my last go at the jury and I was pretty well stuck and satisfied with the seated jury.

Outside, in lovely Bington, it was heavy-leaf summer, July golfing time. Inside, the courtroom was paneled in dark wood that had grown darker down a hundred-plus years. It was a Bington lawyer legend that the ghosts of dead judges and lawyers convened there nightly, overruling each other for fun and frivolity. The courtroom was now air-conditioned, but on a warm summer day it was hard to tell it. Watching the squirrels in their effortless play, I'd figured enviously that it must be cooler outside than in.

I stood up. There's a teetery lectern the judge allows attorneys to use in jury trials. I walked to it and leaned carefully on it and dallied a bit with my notes. Behind me I heard Judge Harner sigh.

"Each of you now seated have sat through this agony for several days. You've heard me ask bright, intelligent questions and Mr. Leaks raise ridiculous objections," I said, smiling, but only at the jury.

"Your honor," Leaks protested, rising.

I smiled some more at the jury. "I'll withdraw that. You've heard Mr. Leaks describe this as a capital case, heaven knows why . . ."

Leaks was up again. This time his voice was louder. "Your honor."

"Get on with it, Mr. Robak," the judge said softly. "Let's leave argument, sarcasm, and your attempts at humor for the proper time, if such ever occurs."

I nodded at Judge Harner and then at Leaks. Leaks had brought one of his deputies with him, a young one, dewy-eyed, long-haired, gung ho for the state and fresh out of law school. His name was Ellison and Herman was impressed because he'd gone to "Hahvud." I had an idea Deputy Ellison was nudging him now and then, making decisions for him. Leaks needed that. He was vicious, unswift, and, worst of all, untrustworthy. At one time I'd tentatively dealt the case we were trying for a twenty-year sentence on a lesser, included offense, but word of it had sifted out before we could paper-finalize it. The local media reports, partially influenced by the deceased's large family, had been most unkind. Leaks was running for a third term. Suddenly he'd denied stoutly any bargain had been offered and pushed for trial. He'd said, "You know how it is, Don. I deal this one and they'll chew my butt for breakfast." He'd cocked his head and looked out at me with wandering eyes.

"I'll make it up to you," he'd promised.

"It isn't me, Herman. It's my client." I'd smiled, but only a little. "You want a war. You got a war. I don't like it when anyone backs out on a proffered deal."

I doubted Leaks would get the death penalty. The case seemed routine. Ed Sager had threatened Beth Sager in front of witnesses numerous times and they'd battled in public, but there were enough peculiarities about both her death and her mode of living prior to death that I didn't think a jury would recommend the death penalty. I also doubted my client, Ed Sager, would get off with only twenty years (which really didn't mean twenty years served). He'd made difficulties for himself. He had, at least by what he'd said in several peculiar statements, killed his wife Beth with a .38 Hy Hunter derringer.

I smiled once more for the jurors and got down to business. "Is there anyone among you twelve who, knowing your own state of mind now, would hesitate to try this case because he or she feels they couldn't be fair to the defendant?" I looked the twelve over. "How about you, Mr. McNear? Do you trust yourself to be a fair juror?"

The Number One Juror, a sturdy farmer who'd once been on the county council, nodded stolidly at me.

"Mr. Turner? Mrs. Larrance?"

I got nods or yesses all the way down the line. They were ring-wise. Someplace along the line each of the survivors had decided it would be "all right" to be a juror, unlike the hordes who'd not wanted to serve.

I picked up my papers and went back to my table and sat down. My client, my long-ago, one-time-close but cuckolded friend, sat apathetically watching. His full name was Edwin Lewis Sager and he was five years or so younger than my forty-four. He looked ten years older.

"Jury okay with you, Ed?" I asked in a whisper.

He shrugged, not giving a damn. He was the first man I'd ever represented who truly wanted to die. I'd had a few who'd carried on the death wish pretense for a time, but the rest had recovered their balance in time for trial. Ed hadn't.

I'd met Ed when I'd first arrived in Bington, drawn the contracts when he opened his original variety store, settled his first wife's estate when she'd died in a wreck on 421, and been best man at his second marriage. Later I'd officiated informally at some of his frequent marital breakups and bedded his lovely, amoral wife when I'd been called to her house one lonely night before my Jo. I'd finally given up on Ed when heavy social drinking became a full-time sickness with him. His business had suffered because of the drinking and the times. Now, he still had half a dozen stores or so out of the once thirty, but employees had stolen him poor and other lawyers were about ready to pounce in the bankruptcy courts.

I was, sort of, back with him. He wanted to die. He believed I was to officiate at the rites. There had to be a trial before he could die unless he could find a quicker way. He'd tried suicide in jail once with pills and done a wretched job. He'd then reluctantly agreed with his seventeen-year-old son from marriage one and with his older, fiftyish brother to hire me. Ed's relationship with me was, at best, fragile.

"Sure, okay," he said, not looking at me or the jury.

I rose. "Defendant accepts the jury."

Judge Harner smiled for the first time in several days, new life in his eyes. He was a bulldog of a man, impatient, but able enough as a trial judge.

Several reporters got up hastily in the back of the courtroom and headed for the doors. The case had been heavily covered and, for a time early in it, Leaks and I had traded daily bulletins until Judge Harner, tiring of it, had slapped a gag order on both of us.

The twenty or so remaining prospective petit jurors, seeing the newspeople rise, thought things were done. A few of them also rose tentatively.

"Those of you called for jury duty will please resume your seats," Judge Harner ordered. "We have a jury, but now we'll add two alternates to it." He dug down below his bench and came up with a worn bench book. "You twelve jurors stand up and raise your right hands."

The jury shuffled to their feet looking self-consciously at each other.

"Do you and each of you swear or affirm under the pains and penalties of perjury that you will well and truly try the case of the *State* v. *Edwin Sager?* Those of you who swear, so help you God, and those of you who affirm do so under the pains and penalties of perjury." He prompted them. "All say I will."

They choroused it obediently for him. I looked them over once more, both satisfied and dissatisfied, but then it was always that way with final jury selections in any of my trials I could remember. Jury selection is not a completely scientific process. This one had Juror Number One McNear, whom I'd wanted, plus another dirt farmer. There were two farm wives from out in north county, two teachers, one of them a male oldster from the university and the other a demure, young female English teacher from South High. There were three variously aged housewives, one thirtyish laid-off male factory worker who'd seemed glad to be called, and, lastly, two downtown businessmen whose sense of duty seemed momentarily to have overwhelmed their natural cupidity. Besides, it was summer and most of the students had fled. Slack time in Bington. Hell, serve on the jury. Make a good thing to talk about at Kiwanis.

"Be back in the jury room at nine in the morning on Monday," Judge Harner ordered. "Bailiff, when I'm done, show them out through the jury room so they'll know where to return. During the time you jurors are out of this courtroom you'll not discuss the matter here in trial among yourselves or with any other person, read or listen to any media accounts concerning it, or form any opinion on it until you've heard all the evidence, the final arguments of counsel, and the final instructions of the court. I don't want any of you, in plainer words, doing any weekend research on the case, talking about it with friends or relatives, or reading newspaper accounts concerning it, or listening and watching other media accounts." He nodded to his bailiff.

We waited the jury out. When the last of them had vanished down the dark hall outside the courtroom we quite quickly, in less than an hour, picked two alternate jurors.

I walked back to the jail with Ed Sager and a quiet but watchful uniformed deputy.

"It'll take all of Monday morning to hear the preliminary instructions and make opening statements," I said to Sager, making conversation.

He smiled gently at me. "Why all this bother, Don? I've confessed. They've got my little pocket gun and my prints are on it. We've been fighting with each other for years, Beth and me. You know that. You officiated informally enough. I know Beth used to cry on your shoulder when I'd go off on a drunk."

I nodded, a little embarrassed at the memory. It had been on one of those occasions that things had gotten out of hand. A long time ago.

"Can't I just plead guilty?" he asked.

"It's not that easy, Ed," I said, talking as if I were talking with a small child. "You don't remember what happened. Your various statements show that." I watched him. He seemed lost in some faraway place. "Do you remember shooting Beth?"

He hesitated and I thought, for a moment, he was again going to say he did remember. He'd tried that once early on and made such a botch of it that I'd soon had him admitting he remembered little of Beth's final day. He'd also admitted he'd been drunk, mad, vengeful, and afterward suicidal that day. The county police had found him trying to fire the defective part of a two-shot derringer into his own head. I had a young psychiatrist who'd treated him starting long before Beth's death who was willing to testify that he'd been insane at the time of the murder, that the blackout, the loss of memory were real. My evidence would also show both his long addiction to alcohol and his state of intoxication on the day Beth Sager died. Intoxication and insanity aren't very good defenses, but they were what I had. They were also all I did have except some sympathy for Ed, my own talent for confusion, and some dirt on his deceased wife. Confucius say when law on your side then beat on law, when facts on your side, beat on facts. When neither on your side, beat on table. *Table Robak.*

In this case beating on tables and threatening to widen the case into an inquiry into Beth's past with some of Bington's best people had been my best move.

"I've told you what little I remember of that day," Ed said.

"Okay. Whether you like it or not the law says if you kill someone while insane then you aren't legally responsible for the death. You go to a hospital instead of a prison." We crossed the asphalt parking lot and I motioned the deputy to a stop outside the jail door. A tree above us shaded the sun and there was a fine, cool breeze. "Look around at the world, Ed. Try to remember what it was like to be out of jail. You're dried out now. Maybe this time you could stop drinking. Try to think about how she cheated you and drove you where you are now. Think also about how good it would be to be free again. If you go to a mental hospital they'll treat you for a time and eventually release you. I promise you that's the way it happens." I shook my head. "If you'd done as I first advised and not made so many statements we might also have defended on the grounds she committed suicide, but that's gone now. I don't want you to lie on the witness stand if you testify."

"I want to testify," he said, focusing on me again. "I will testify."

"All right," I said soothingly. I thought I knew what he planned to do. Once on the stand he'd confess all over again, this time for his jury. "I don't want any lies from the witness stand," I said again. "I want you to fight back from there. I don't want any suicidal fantasies. You know I'll find them out and make you tell the truth. Try to get yourself to want to stay alive, get yourself cured, and out of this mess."

For a tiny instant I thought I had him a little with me, but then he smiled vaguely up at the green trees over us and turned the smile to the tall deputy who'd taken it all in and who'd surely pass on every word to the prosecutor.

Silent loafers watched us curiously from the brick and stone wall that fronted the jail. It was summer, loafer time. I saw a wine bottle being covertly passed. I sighed and wished momentarily I'd not taken Ed Sager's case. Sometimes, particularly in summer, I'd thought I'd make a better loafer-bum than a lawyer-bum. I tolerated alcohol well, I liked idle talk, and I was a first-class whittler.

A loafer waved to Ed. "Stay with it, Ed," he called.

I nodded. "Some of the town's on your side, Ed."

Ed Sager smiled. "You know who that is, Don?"

I shook my head.

"That's just another drunk like me. The only reason he'd ever want me out is for me to buy him a drink."

"I see."

"Good old Don," Ed said. He patted my shoulder as if I was the one on trial for my life and he was my comforter. He looked over at the deputy and sniffed at the cool breeze. "Feels more like September than July. Hunting season. Take me on inside, Arny."

"I'd like to talk some more," I said.

"Monday's soon enough," Sager said. "Inside, Arny."

Arny opened the door and the smells from inside overwhelmed the smells from outside. The air coming from the jail smelled of sweat and urine and stale, rotting food.

I sourly watched them through the door. Ed was a tall man, but he was bowed a little now. When I'd been best man at his second marriage to Beth people had said enviously that the best-looking, most eligible man in Bington was marrying the most beautiful girl in town. Now Beth was dead and I'd seen and soon a jury would see her unpretty, final pictures, bullet hole and all. To counteract those pictures I had a few of my own of Beth in a white bathing suit, Beth on a horse, Beth in a long, clinging dress.

Ed had now lost most of his hair and some of his teeth to time and liquor. His chain of variety-grocery stores, which had made him small-town rich for a while, seemed a poor return for what the years had purloined from him. The two of them, Ed and Beth, had lived and loved together for a time and then fallen away from each other. She'd then used his plush house, his swimming pool, his good whiskey, and his long absences for her several lovers while Ed had, for a while, pursued more dollars to clink against those he already possessed. Now, even the dollars were gone and Beth was dead. *To each his own.*

The thing which was puzzling was that Ed had known she had lovers. I thought, uncomfortably, he might even have known I was temporarily one of them a long time back. He'd not gone over the edge before. I wondered why suddenly he had, if he had. I still thought it was a slim possibility he'd found her dead and then gone into his present act. I knew he didn't remember killing her. The psychiatrist, young Dr. William Lee Tyne, had talked to me knowingly about pressure-cooker living and how things must have built up slowly to a boil inside Ed Sager. He'd told me learnedly about blackouts and the blocking away of hated memories. It had all sounded clinical and correct, if difficult to sell to a jury, when I'd heard him explain the same things to a smiling, unbelieving but respectful prosecutor during his deposition.

I knew the prosecutor would present many lay witnesses to testify Ed Sager was sane and acting normally and as usual before the murder. There were also two psychiatrists appointed by the court who'd examined Ed and whose testimony concerning him wasn't completely favorable. I'd seen their reports.

I knew another thing Herman Leaks would undoubtedly do come Monday morning. He'd draw up an empty chair by his counsel table and tell the jury that was the chair for the absent witness, the deceased victim, who couldn't be present in court, but who cried out from the grave for justice. He'd done it before. It was cornball, but jurors see only one case, so it was effective. I thought about ways to combat his "absent witness." One came and I smiled inwardly.

Crooked shyster Table Robak.

CHAPTER TWO

Steinmetz's law: "A trial's like it is when you're playing bridge or hearts, Don. When somebody's long then somebody's short."

I walked back to the office. It was late enough on thank-God-it's-Friday so that all the secretaries had fled. Jake's office was dark. So was Sam King's, our muscular new associate, but there was a light on in Steinmetz's office. I stuck my head in his door. On the wall behind where he sat he'd hung an ornate sign. It read, "Old Age and Treachery Will Overcome Youth and Skill." I'd asked him several times who'd made it for him, but he'd only grunted and gone on to some other topic.

He was reading advance sheets of recently decided appellate cases. He did his reading as no one else did. Most lawyers, me included, skim advance sheets, looking for radical changes, drawn here and there by random headnotes. Steinmetz read every word and could quote opinions back twenty years later at need. He wasn't much at long trials because he no longer had the stomach or stamina for them, but he was great to take along to help during the heart and heat portion of a trial, civil or criminal. Judge Harner, who'd unexpectedly beaten him in a primary two years back and therefore retired him, had immense respect for him. When Steinmetz quoted law you could almost see Harner's head nodding. It made a few opposing lawyers angry and insecure, but that bothered neither Steinmetz nor Harner. Their mutual admiration society was exclusive. Steinmetz had never complained after his defeat and told everyone who'd listen that Harner was a "good judge" and had first-class "judicial temperament." That was high recommendation because it came from someone the bar recognized as having been the best of judges.

"Get your jury?" he asked. I knew he'd been waiting for me. He had his feet up on his desk and he was chewing an unlit cigar.

"Ten minutes ago," I said.

"Who'd you get?"

I read the names. Earlier we'd gone over the panel and he'd told me things about most of them. He knew almost everyone, and there was, within him, a switch he could turn on at will for recall. Days long gone were separate entities to him and he remembered all of them. It was a fearsome gift for he also must remember totally the sad moments, the long months of pain when his wife lay on her deathbed, his defeats, sicknesses. When he'd left the bench his ulcer had unexpectedly cleared up so that now he spent many of his nights at the downtown Moose with cronies and tall Early Times married to branch water.

Every juror now serving on the jury was someone he'd starred for me.

He listened, now and then nodding approval. One name made him grin widely.

"Gordon McNear? Leaks left McNear on the jury?"

I'd purposely saved McNear's name for last, knowing it would delight Steinmetz.

"Yep. I asked McNear if he'd known either the defendant or the deceased and he said he'd known both of them vaguely. There were others who answered the same way so Leaks never asked McNear any more about it. And McNear came over very law and order. He stayed and stayed and finally got sworn with the rest."

"McNear knew Beth socially much better than he knew Ed," Steinmetz said. He gave me a leer. "When he was into politics, six or eight years ago now, he was hound-dogging every available lady." He nodded. "That would be before your stint with Beth."

"Who told you about Beth and me?" I asked, startled a little.

"I never divulge sources. But she and McNear were more of an item than you were with her. They were thick as spring-thaw molasses for quite a time." He grinned some more. "I know McNear real well. I put him on tax boards a couple of times. He don't do anything without weighing it, eyeing it, fingering it, and thinking lots about it. He's the kind of guy who, if you took him to a baseball game, would come home knowing all the batting averages, what the attendance at the game was, and what every good-looking lady near him in the park had on or off."

"Him knowing her could cut the other way," I said. "He might want to punish Ed for using a gun on sweet Beth."

"I don't think so. I was judge when McNear was on the council. Like I say, I know him. In my opinion he's damned glad she's gone to glory. Now there's no chance of her causing trouble for him. So you've got yourself a juror who knows intimately what she was like alive." He took his feet down from his desk. "When do you want me to come over?"

"Not yet. Monday we'll have preliminary instructions and opening statements plus maybe the sheriff and some of his people. I want to be by myself that day for some tactical reasons. But how about Tuesday?" I nodded, thinking about it. "You coming over might pump up Sager a bit. He's about as low as I've ever seen anyone. He hates himself and all the world. He wants out of it. Maybe if he sees both of us scrapping for him it'll help him." I smiled at Steinmetz. "And more than just helping Ed you'll cause confusion in Leaks's camp. He hates you more than he hates me."

Steinmetz nodded. Leaks did hate him. In his days on the bench Steinmetz had openly detested the prosecutor. Several times I'd heard Steinmetz call Leaks down from the bench for some shabby trick he'd played on a defendant or a member of the bar. Now Steinmetz was defeated, out of office and power, and Leaks was still riding high. It should have been Steinmetz who'd lost, but it wasn't so. Whenever he came to court Steinmetz caused Leaks to have heart problems. I thought it was because Steinmetz was so bright and straight and ethical and Leaks sort of the other way. Leaks wasn't without ability or a certain limited amount of cunning. He was competent and sometimes even savage in court. He could take a line from "A" to "Z." His problem was he might brush close to five letters and miss three while he crossed the rest. Steinmetz could take that same alphabet and write poetry with it.

"Herman needs us to devil him and complicate his life," Steinmetz said, not smiling.

"I suppose."

He remained serious. "It's our town out there, too, Don. I'd rather I contributed to decisions made in it instead of allowing them to be made solely by Herman and other, companion idiots." He nodded. "Murder trials are like morality plays. The murder is the prime violation, but if you or we can find enough counter violations the murder can wind up outweighed."

"Sure, Judge," I said soothingly. Sometimes he got more intense than I thought he ought to get and I'd heard his doctor say those times were bad for him.

He sighed, giving up on me for now.

"You've had some calls," he said. "Our new man in the office served your batch of subpoenas. Sam's too large to argue with and so they waited until he was gone and then called you. Some sounded pretty irate. The list is someplace on your desk."

"I think I'll skip that now. I'll let them sweat it out. I might come down tomorrow and make some calls and, again, I might not. And, as usual, I'll unplug my home phone."

He nodded. "I've seen some of your mail. The girls open it and show me the real dillies. And there have been some phone calls here where the girls had their ears blasted."

I shrugged. Phone calls and crank letters came with murder-defense territory. In addition there were plenty of people out there in the town and county who hated me. I felt all right about that. If they'd liked me I'd have known I was wrong.

"How now, then?" Steinmetz asked. "I'm off soon to the Moose. Care to come along? There'll be insulting talk, dice shaken for drinks, plus a few salacious stories. Good for you—pumps up the blood."

"No. I told my wife I'd meet her for dinner in a sober condition. Her aunt has the baby for the evening. She fights us to get him." I smiled, thinking about my family. I was long in tooth to have one, but I had one anyway. "That makes it nice for Jo and gets us out some. Jo played golf this afternoon." I looked up at the clock on Steinmetz's wall. "She should be about to finish the ninth hole by the time I arrive. Dr. Billy Tyne and his latest are going to meet us for dinner."

"That's the psychiatrist?"

"That's our psychiatrist. The judge appointed his two, but they're not strong for our side. Tyne has seen and treated Ed Sager, mostly for alcoholism. He also counseled Ed and Beth in their marital difficulties. Without Tyne our chances slip from slim to none."

Steinmetz shook his head. "When's the last time you heard about either an insanity defense or an intoxication defense walking a defendant out of court?" He smiled his charming, bald-headed smile, the wrinkles from it spreading all the way back to his neckline. "Only dumb bastards like thee think you can get a man off who admits killing his beautiful, unfaithful wife, wants to die, and keeps making incriminating statements to every uniform who passes his cell. Sometimes I wonder if he's faking us. I had a court-appointed case once where my lad tried faking insanity. A fellow inmate in jail conned him into it, clued him on the symptoms, and then appeared against him to testify for some promised time off." He sighed. "My client was still in last I heard and that was years later."

"That's not Ed Sager," I said. "He's not faking. He's so depressed you've got to dig him out of the ground to show him the sun."

"Are you pushing so hard for him because of an old, but guilty conscience?"

"I hope not," I said, not completely sure. "My time with Beth was over almost before it started. Defending Ed's just business."

"You'll look good if you can get him past the death penalty after all the prosecutor's news releases."

"I'd rather get him by with a short term on an included offense."

"You mean less than the twenty Leaks offered once?"

"Yes."

He shook his head. "Dream on."

I drove down to the Bington Country Club. Children played exuberant water tag in an antiseptic-looking blue pool. The parking lot was full of Lincolns, Cadillacs, foreign sports cars, and big, polished station wagons. I parked my drab LTD in an open spot.

I walked around to the back of the club. There was a patio back there. Huge trees shaded it. It was a great day, even though much of it was now gone. The temperature had to be no more than seventy-five and there was a fine, light breeze.

I could see Jo on the eighth hole. She was playing with three of her golfing friends in the Friday night ladies' league. I waved, but she was too far away to see me.

I went in and got a Tab. Later there might be V.O. and tall water, but for now, a Tab was good. Jo had cleaned up my drinking bad habits a mite. There'd been a lot of years when those habits had needed extensive repair work. Now I drank sparingly.

I took my Tab and went back out. Jo had driven off the tee and was approaching the ninth green. Her second shot was short of the green. She pitched on, then two-putted for a bogie. She made a face at me. She looked so trim and lovely I could only smile.

"Couldn't putt tonight to save me," she said, shaking her head. She took the Tab from my hand and sipped it. "Mmmmmmmmm."

"You can have all you want. It's a diet drink," I said gravely, squeezing her arm. "Won't fatten you up."

She looked me over and her dark eyes danced. "Hard day in court?"

"Medium. I kept three-putting all my objections. And Herman Leaks complained some of my questions were out of bounds and a hazard to the legal profession."

She handed me back the Tab abruptly. "I'll leave you here to mutter that kind of nonsense to yourself while I go shower. See you in the bar in a while?"

I nodded. "Don't forget we're having dinner with Dr. Tyne," I reminded.

Something passed quickly over her face like a small cloud crossing the sun. Her face was normally very calm and serene and—happy. She didn't like doctors as a group or singly, but she put up with them.

"Do you have something against the good doctor?" I asked.

"He's good-looking," she said. "He pinched me once."

"You never told me that. He'll have his latest along with him tonight. I think she's a nurse or something. He'll be pinching her."

"I'd bet on that," she said.

I gave her a small, quick kiss and added a pinch. She tapped my knee with her putter. "None of that on the golf course, buster."

I watched her out of sight and then went back inside the club and got another Tab.

Around me the Friday nightlife of small-town Bington began to roar. People drank too much and smoked too much and yelled smilingly at each other so as to be heard over the din. I listened to golfers telling lies and truths at the bar. A group of Friday night lady golfers sat drinking around a center table. I recognized some of the ladies and resolved to be careful. Beth, Ed Sager's deceased wife, had been Bington-born and was related to many in town. She'd come from a proud, old family. She'd gone to school mostly in local schools and then graduated from the local university. There, I remembered, she'd been big-time sorority and a homecoming queen. She'd been beautiful. Some people related to her were now very death-blind to her faults, which they'd whispered about before her death. Now that she was dead, and Ed had killed her, they loudly wanted his head. They also wanted no one tarnishing her memory in the process. I knew it was rumored I planned to do precisely that and I did plan it.

A lady got up from the middle table and lurched my way. She was carrying her drink. Her face was grim. Her name was Ann Jellicoe. She was Beth's cousin. Her name was also on Herman Leaks's witness list, one of a group of relatives and friends he'd indicated he might call. I knew her a little from the club, fund drives, and mixed golf. She prided herself on her sharp tongue. I'd heard her boast loudly about people she'd put to rout. She was fiftyish, stout, and could sometimes hit a golf ball a long way. She also complained about every shot. She was a sour woman whose life was made up of endless bridge games, screwdrivers (healthy, you know), and golf, golf, golf.

"How goes the trial?" she asked, her face twisting a bit.

"Hasn't begun yet," I said.

"Poor, dear Beth. People say Ed's now full of repentance and sits up in jail wanting to die." She looked around and saw she had an audience so she raised her voice. "You lawyers won't let him do that, will you?" She gave me a hard, small smile.

"Suicide's illegal," I said mildly.

"So's murder, but some people, lawyers particularly, don't seem to know it."

"We know it. The difference is that lawyers recognize degrees of guilt, insanity . . ."

"Insanity? Degrees of guilt? He killed her with his gun and that's that."

"Do you really think so?"

"Everyone does," she said. "Everyone, but you."

I smiled some more. Perhaps it would pass. "Well, there's also a jury. I understand you're to be a witness. I didn't get around to interviewing you. Maybe I should do that now."

She nodded. "I'm going to tell how he threatened to kill her and then did kill her," she said venomously. "I'm going to tell a lot of things that won't help drunken Ed Sager."

"Are you now?" I asked, seemingly fascinated.

"Any decent lawyer would have pled him guilty long ago," she said. "But not you, Robak, not you. The town knows about you. File anything for a buck, do anything for two."

Things had gone from loud to quiet in the bar. It was time to stop listening. I considered just getting up and walking away, but I thought she'd probably follow along.

"Let's see, Ann, you'd be a little too old to have done any double-running with Beth, wouldn't you? But you won't mind if I ask you about that on cross-examination?"

Her face went dark in surprise and rage. "I ought to throw this drink on you."

I smiled at her, which made her angrier. "I've not been hired by you or your deceased cousin's relatives. I've been hired by Ed's people. Whether you like it or not, whether anyone likes it or not, I'll be in court doing my job."

"You're a true son of a bitch," she said. "You're a grave despoiler. This town knows you're a cheap shyster, Robak."

"I don't know you well enough to return your compliments, lady. All I can say about you now is that you have a bad backswing and a loud, dirty mouth."

She threw her drink at me. I'd thought she might and she telegraphed it. I stepped aside. Most of the drink landed on her long-suffering, bandbox husband, who was coming up behind me to see what was going on. He looked at me and then at her, tiny mustache working, ready to cry. I remembered he'd run once for public office years back, a minor thing, a township advisory board. He'd run dead last. I'd thought then it was more her fault than his. He seemed pleasant enough.

"Best shot you probably made all day," I said to her.

Someone at her center table laughed nervously.

"Don't get close to me again," she screamed, all sanity gone. "If we were on the golf course I'd take a two iron to you."

"You'd shank it."

"I'll shank you, shyster. And I'll shank Ed too." Her hands shook.

I smiled. "Let's make this the last words between us, except in court."

She had a handkerchief out and was wiping hard at her husband's clothes. He had on a white jacket, light checked pants, shirt and tie, and white shoes. The orange juice from her screwdriver seemed to have gotten well dispersed. Her handkerchief was spreading the damage.

I could see resolve steady his quivering chin. "You want to step outside?" he whispered tentatively.

"If it'll make you feel better," I answered. "You want to freshen up first or go now. Orange juice at thirty paces maybe? Vodka optional?"

She put a husky, restraining arm around him. "Remember your bad back." She used the handkerchief roughly. "Forget the louse."

I let her have that additional last word and went over and sat down at the bar. The bartender grinned at me and I turned my back on the Jellicoes. I nodded at the bartender coolly. I'd made at least a part of whatever reputation I had in town by being a prickly maverick. I had no intention of letting Beth Sager's relatives walk over me while the trial was on or keep me from going where I wanted to be. I'd have put up with an oblique attack, but not a frontal one. I thought maybe this one might be the last. Surely some of Beth's relatives realized she'd not been perfect? I sat at the bar and figured darkly that Ann Jellicoe had probably let a bad golf game and a few quick screwdrivers, plus her notorious temper, get the best of her.

Jo tapped me on the shoulder.

"How about a table?" she asked.

I smiled and nodded. I followed her tamely out of the bar. Behind me I could hear Ann Jellicoe's voice increase in volume and venom as I left the field of battle to her.

Jo led me into the main dining room. Photographs of racehorses and race cars lined the walls, mingled with pictures of local golf champs holding their cups high and smiling condescendingly at each other. Air-conditioned breezes huffed from window vents. Outside the windows birds flew in circles looking for a tree to sleep in.

"Thanks for the rescue," I said, thinking Jo would not know what I meant.

She nodded. "I heard about it almost before you did. One of the ladies at the center table played in my foursome this afternoon. Before it started she came hurrying downstairs where I was dressing and told me to come up and protect you. Ann Jellicoe had already told around on the course that if you showed up here tonight she was going to make it hot for you. She cheats on her score, you know. Either that or she has a very poor memory and she does seem to remember other things all right." She smiled at me and I was warmed by it. "Ann also said around that I was all right and my only problem was having a bastard like you for a husband."

"True," I admitted.

"You seem to have fared all right. No scratches, no bruises. Did you dump the drink on Chuck Jellicoe?"

"Nope. His sweetums-pie did that, although it probably won't come out that way after it gets told a time or two. The drink was meant for me, but her backswing, as usual, was off and she shanked it. She first tried to tell me off, but I didn't respond tamely to it." I smiled to show I didn't mean it. "I might serve her with a subpoena in case Herman doesn't call her."

"She's half bear, but a gentleman lawyer would just have let her tell him off." She shook her head, but I thought I could see a gleam of approval in her eyes. I wasn't sure. Sometimes she wasn't that much in favor of my profession.

"I guess I'm not a gentleman lawyer," I admitted gravely. "I do have a ladylike wife."

One of the golfing ladies who'd been sitting at the table with Ann Jellicoe picked that moment to come past our table. She patted me on the shoulder gingerly and leaned close. "Good for you, Robak," she whispered. She looked around to make certain she was unnoticed and then scurried away.

"Did you ever consider that maybe one of Beth's male relatives might get irritated at you?" Jo asked severely. "There are probably lots of large, young ones. It's an old Bington family."

I shrugged. "I'm not mad at Beth, Jo. She's dead and I'm sorry she's dead, but my job is Ed. I'm his advocate, bought and partially paid for. No large, bearish Beth relative, male or female, will stop me from being his advocate. That's how my profession works."

"How well I know," she said, smiling a little.

CHAPTER THREE

Ann. Statutes: Expert witnesses may testify to beliefs or opinions after they have been properly qualified.

When Dr. Tyne and his date came we ordered a drink with them. Jo, after years of total abstinence, had finally arrived at a time in her life when she could have a Tom Collins or two without believing she was being revisited with original sin. Her first husband had been a professional alcoholic and she'd married me knowing I also drank. It had been a hard choice for her. For a time she'd watched me carefully. When I'd not cursed her, beaten her, or stolen from her purse she'd slowly thawed to my drinking. And I had, knowing her fears, become more moderate in my habit until that habit had become moderate.

We'd mellowed together.

Doc Tyne's latest lady was spectacular. She was a physical-looking blonde named Alice and she was, she said, a nurse. I figured her age at about twenty-five to thirty. When she walked everything had movement. It jiggled or made interesting waves. She had people at nearby tables craning to watch. She had a little-girl voice and she simpered rather than laughed. She drank Beefeater martinis with a peel straight up with rapid frequency and great gusto. Tyne drank V.O. and water, like me.

"How goes it?" Tyne asked, when things had quieted down.

"We got our jury late today. The trial should take about a week. I'll call you ahead of time so you'll know when you're going on." I thought of something. "You've testified before?"

"Yes. A number of times."

"The way it'll work in this one is that near the end of the trial the judge will call and himself examine the court-appointed psychiatrists. His final question will be whether or not Ed Sager was, on the nineteenth day of March, insane. Both the state and the defense get to cross-examine those witnesses called by the court and also call rebuttal witnesses. Unless I decide to call you before, you'll be my rebuttal witness."

He nodded. "Okay. I could almost smell trouble coming for them. He stopped coming around. She continued. I saw her in my office a couple of days before she died."

I knew that from the deposition, but I nodded.

"She was into problems herself. She was coming up on menopause time."

"Tell me about that."

"She ran highs and lows. A lot of her life was sex. She thought it would end at menopause. I kept trying to convince her life wasn't that way. I'd get the job done and/or she'd fall in love with someone new and it would be okay for a time. Then she'd lose the faith. She'd find a gray hair, a wrinkle."

"She did a lot of running," I said. It was something we both knew.

He nodded.

"Nymphomania?"

He shook his head. "Not that. She liked men and sex. Nymphomaniacs don't. Her attitude to sex was more male than female. She was a seduction planner. She liked to play games. She could waste a whole day planning something, doing her puzzles, and watching herself in the mirror. She knew she could go out to a bar or a club and pick someone up about anytime she wanted, but that wasn't her normal operation. She liked to plan ahead. She liked intimate pool parties, romance, and light-on-the-booze drinks. She wanted her lovers to love her and love is hard to find and keep these days. She was selective, but the pill set her free." He gave me a questioning look. "She told me once she plotted and came after you a long time ago."

I nodded. It had been long before Jo and I were married. Beth had been then a fantastic-looking woman, very bright and bubbly. She'd asked me to come to the house and talk with her about Ed and his problems during one of their many breakups. I'd gone. I'd found her by the pool in a little white bathing suit that made her look almost nude. I'd soon peeled her willingly out of that.

"Call me and come over and swim again," she'd said gently when I'd left hours later.

Many times and for a long time I'd been tempted to go back. She'd even called once or twice. But there was Ed. I'd dropped him as a close friend when he became a practicing, devout drunk, but he still was a part of my town and life. Going into his home and getting into bed with his wife without premeditation was bad enough, going there with plans was worse.

Then Jo came along.

I almost missed Doc's next, musing remark. "She started keeping a diary on things about a year or two ago. She showed it to me once, but she wouldn't let me read it. She just waved it in front of me and told me I ought to be in it. I told her to burn it. Later, she said she had."

"A book? You never said anything to me or in the deposition about a book. Jesus, Bill."

"I thought I told you about that," he said, not caring much. "I'm sure I mentioned it. Besides, even if I didn't, she said she'd burned it."

I shook my head excitedly and he saw it.

"Try the house. It would have to be someplace there if it still exists. Maybe her bedroom." He thought for a moment. "I was at the house when she showed it to me."

My mind moved into high gear. If there was a book around with names in it, events in it, I might be able to do several things with it. First off, I could show it to Ed Sager. It might make him mad. It might make him want to fight back a little. Second, I'd already supplied Herman Leaks with my witness list during discovery, but I could still supplement the list. All it gave Leaks, if I did supplement at this late time, was a right to a continuance where I could show the evidence and the witness names were newly discovered. Third, if there were names in her book of those in the Bington money or political power structure, I could be back at my twenty-year deal (or less), if Ed Sager would accept the deal. Herman Leaks was a politician. He'd backed off some originally when I'd served my witness list on him because there were witnesses on it he owed political favors, witnesses whose support he must have to get reelected. The book could be additional evidence, could implicate those already named, allowing me to ask them probing questions, a paper thing I could hand to the jury so they could finger it and frown and realize the depths of Beth's perfidy.

"How about you, Doc? You know about me. Were you immune to Beth?" I asked the question in a low voice so the girls wouldn't hear.

He looked oddly at me. "I was a constant, never-ending project with her. The only thing that kept me out of her bed was the fact I was counseling both Ed and Beth plus there's this old duck named Hippocrates." He smiled. "Not that I'd not have liked to hop in. Hell, Hippocrates might have also. Once she called me to come to the house and when I walked out there she was wearing a robe. I thought maybe she'd not had time to dress, but that wasn't it. I came into the house and she took the robe off and posed for a moment and then I had a lot of woman hanging all over me." He shook his head. "I left."

I smiled at the story. Before Jo I'd done some late-night running and partying with him. He drew girls like syrup draws flies. He'd been married a couple of times and marriage had not taken with him. He'd said to me several times that he'd never marry again, but I'd heard the line before. When we'd kicked around together I'd soon been surprised to find I was the dominant personality. The marriages and perhaps the pressures of his job made him oddly insecure, willing to be led. I'd ordered and planned, he'd carried out the plans and orders.

That time had passed.

He'd tried, halfheartedly, to talk me out of marrying Jo. I thought that was one reason she wasn't fond of him. When talking to me hadn't worked he'd continued to call me now and then, usually late, after marriage, for parties. He wasn't very devious about it and I'd shrugged it off. I liked him, but being married had made me like him with reservations.

An attentive waitress brought salads and warm, homemade bread. She lit the candles on the table because it was now almost full dark outside. Later she brought prime rib, twice-baked potatoes, and hot strong coffee. In the far corner of the big room a trio of older men played good music, piano, bass, and guitar.

I ate sparingly and drank less. Jo did also.

Alice turned to me when she'd cleaned her plate. "So you're the great lawyer? Bill talks some about you. You send him business for his marriage clinic." She smiled whitely, her teeth even and sharp. The rest of her equipment seemed to move and vibrate even while she was sitting. "He likes you."

"I like him," I said simply.

She nodded calculatingly. She reached under the table and patted my leg high up.

"I met him through his clinic," she said. "My now ex-husband and I went to see him and he tried hard to counsel us, but it didn't work out. Martin was always a bastard." She looked at me and smiled. "Know what I did the day the divorce was granted two weeks ago?"

I shook my head. Her fingers wandered idly and warmly about on my leg.

"I called up Doc Bill," she said triumphantly. "I took him out for dinner and then home to bed with me again like a trophy I'd won." Her voice was medium loud. Other diners watched and listened. "I like trophies. No one is ever going to domesticate this girl again."

Bill and Jo had ceased their conversation. Bill was smiling a small smile. Jo wasn't. Spoilsport.

I got up abruptly from the table. "I'm going to the boy's powder room," I said, borrowing a phrase I'd heard often before, but changing gender.

One of the things I liked best about my Saturday middle-life mornings was that when I awoke I had no hangover.

I edged silently out of bed. In the crib in the far corner of our bedroom young Joseph Thomas Robak slept soundly. He was a good baby that way. His mother opened one eye at me and watched me slip into running clothes. She beckoned to me after I was dressed.

"You're not going to her?" she asked, not yet smiling about it. "For a time last night I thought she might suggest a foursome."

"I wonder if Doc put her up to it?" I asked. "He's capable of doing that for funzies."

"He pinched me again."

"A friendly pinch or a punishment pinch?" I asked innocently. "He's never forgiven you for removing me from his fun and games."

"This one was a Don-isn't-watching pinch. Kind of sexless."

I tousled her hair. The night, after my return to the dinner table, had disintegrated into now half-remembered shards of voices and laughter. We'd moved to the bar. I'd gone wisely back to Tab. Someone had loudly told the story about my earlier problems with Ann Jellicoe and all those remaining late seemed to be her sworn, lifelong enemies. I'd listened, sipping Tab, while her pedigree was dissected. Doc Tyne and Alice switched to stingers. Jo remained close, also drinking Tab, and protecting my legs and maybe my body from Alice. On a silent, bright screen above the bar the Reds played out a lackluster eleven-inning loss to the Braves.

Eventually I got to do a little of what I'd set up the dinner to accomplish. I talked with Doc about my defense of Ed Sager. I scribbled down questions he told me to try on unfriendly lay witnesses and also the two court-appointed psychiatrists. As things got louder and they fell deeper into the stingers I set up a lunch with him, no Alice or Jo, later in the week at the downtown Moose. By that time I'd know better what questions Herman Leaks was leaning into and could pick at Doc's brain accordingly.

I ran my five miles in the muggy morning. There's a path I use. It's along the river and primarily it's a biker's path, but in July bicyclists don't seem to be early Saturday risers. I had the path alone. No dogs, no people. Below me the river smelled of dead fish. Tiny waves broke idly on a beach littered with driftwood and beer cans and no-return bottles.

I pounded my way down the path, hoping I looked to be a brave, solitary runner. My weight was a few pounds above what I wanted it to be, but I figured it'd be back to normal in another week, near or at trial's end. Running let me eat what I wanted as long as I remained careful with alcoholic intake.

I kept thinking about Beth Sager's *maybe* diary. I remembered I'd asked Ed if she'd ever kept a something-like-that, but he'd either not known or told. Trials had made me respect the written word, anything that could be marked, identified, and then passed to a curious jury. I knew some of the people Beth had been seeing. In a small town, you do. *But a diary . . .*

The big house where Beth and Ed had lived had served its police purpose and was now closed and locked. For a time, after Beth's death, it had been closed by court order, but all photos and measurements and the like had been completed and that time had passed. Now, there was an agreement signed by the bank, as Beth's administrator, and Ed allowing the house to be sold, if a sale for it could be managed. A guardian, Giles Sager, had been appointed for Ed Jr., Ed's seventeen-year-old son by his first wife. Giles had also agreed to the sale. The house was legally owned half by Beth's estate and half by Ed. Ed couldn't inherit from Beth's estate if he was convicted. Still, half was his.

As I ran I tried also to remember the details of the listing contract, but not much came to me.

I finished my five miles back at the house Jo and I had jointly bought after our marriage. It was a nice house, three bedrooms, two baths, trees in back and front. It was brick and frame and now about sixty years old, new for downtown Bington, where many of the houses had been built long before the Civil War.

I'd worked up a good sweat so I showered, running it first hot, then cold. Soon I felt human again.

I went out and plugged in the phone jack, which I'd pulled out late last night.

While I was running and showering, Ed Sager, in his cell in the Bington-Mojeff County jail, had tried hard to hang himself with strips torn from his thin sheet. I found that out about eight, while Jo and I were having our soft-boiled eggs and toast and after Joe had enjoyed his morning Gerbers.

The man who called was a deputy. Sheriffs normally delegate authority well. No sheriff likes to be the personal bearer of bad tidings because the sheriff holds a political office. The deputy's name was Chick Ellman and I knew him a little.

"Your client tried to dutch out early this morning, Don," he informed me laconically. "We found him in his cell a while ago.

He'd maybe have got the job done if he was twenty pounds lighter of if he knew schmatz about knots. We had the county doctor up to look at him and Sheriff Abe told me to call and tell you Ed's okay. He tried tearing his sheet to pieces and weaving a rope. Then he hung what he'd made over the bed hook in the ceiling." The deputy laughed a little. "The way them crooked contractors built this jail I'm surprised either the ceiling or the hook held, but they did. The rope didn't. It broke. By the time it did break, Sager was out. The knot was a granny so it slipped and didn't tighten right. Some of the other prisoners, who'd just watched till then without making a sound, started yelling. The drop wasn't enough to break Ed's neck. He'd wrapped the rest of the sheet around his hands and sort of tied them, maybe using his teeth. I'd say, all in all, you could call it a near miss."

"What's his condition now?"

"The county doctor looked him over. He told us to put him in the padded cell. We did. He won't get nothin' done there. I talked to Ed through the little window. He seemed okay. I asked him if he wanted to see you, but he shook his head." He laughed again. "He's real rational now, Don. He even asked for breakfast."

"Does Herman Leaks know?"

"You know we had to call him before we called you, Don."

"Thanks, Chick."

I hung up and told Jo. "That's twice he's tried suicide in jail. The first time he had some pills. Sheriff Abe knows him so I guess they didn't search him good. Anyway, he took all the pills. They were some kind of prescription tranquilizer, a mild one I guess. All he did was sleep eighteen or twenty hours. No one took that one seriously. I wonder what Herman Leaks thinks now?"

Jo watched me, knowing I wasn't done.

"I could ask for a continuance," I said, considering it. "But all that would do is slow things down. It wouldn't help Ed." I shook my head, not knowing what to do. "I'm not sure there's really any way to help Ed."

Jo asked, "What are you going to do now?"

"Ed doesn't want to see me so I'm going to finish the coffee, get dressed again, and go to the office. There I'm going to look up who has the Sager property listed. Then I'm going to go out past the house and do some looking."

She smiled gently. "What for? For your client or for Don Robak?"

"I'm not sure, Jo," I said honestly. "I suppose he's guilty and that his suicide attempts are the result of his intense feeling of guilt. The thing that has me puzzled is he remembers nothing about the killing. I keep running theories through my head where she was dead when he came back to the house and found her. He'd been into the booze a lot, before and after the fact. Maybe she was dead, maybe not. Doc Tyne says people like Sager, people with deep guilt complexes, can hide away from what happened, black it out. I called one of the court-appointed psychiatrists and he said there was no agreement on that among the experts in the area. Some say yes, others say no. But Sager wants to remember so he can confess it too. All he does remember is the body and the blood and the gun and trying to shoot himself, but nothing before. A couple of times he tried to fantasize stories for me about what happened. He messed it up so badly and I caught him in so many inconsistencies that he gave up saying he remembered. Now he says he doesn't know exactly what happened or what set him off, but that he's sure he killed her. He keeps saying that to everyone and, in jail, a majority of his listeners are police officers." I nodded, thinking. "Doc Tyne thought he might get more out of him by hypnosis or sodium pentothal. He wanted us to get Ed brought to Hill Hospital so he could do him there with questions we provided. But hypnosis and pentothal get into legal problems. The other side always claims you suggested the answers. I might have tried it, but Ed decided not to cooperate." I shook my head. "Maybe he's afraid of finding out, afraid of living Beth's death again. Doc didn't think we'd get anything anyway. He says his opinion is there's a ninety-nine percent chance that there's just nothing else there. So we decided the one percent left wasn't worth us tampering with Ed. Maybe he'll decide to fight back. If he does, and we've hypnotized him or used drugs on him, then what he testifies about will be suspect and a jury would probably believe what he confessed before the fact." I shook my head once more. "But I keep thinking there's an outside possibility someone else could have killed Beth."

"You always think it was someone else," she said fondly. "And you're getting paranoid again. You pulled the plug out of the phone last night and didn't plug it in again until just before your call."

I nodded soberly. "I've subpoenaed some people to testify and they aren't very happy with me. I don't want to argue with them on the phone and I don't want them harassing you. I may call one or more of them from the office phone today. You leave the phone unplugged."

She nodded, not sure about that.

"I guess I'm leery, as maybe I ought to be, when I'm defending someone and the circumstances are as they are in this case. If Ed can remember what happened after then, why can't he remember what happened when Beth died? I keep looking for new facts. If I can find Beth's diary and get copies of it made and served on the prosecutor, if I can subpoena new, sensitive witnesses, I could have Herman backing and nodding and offering the deal he once offered."

"Why's he want the death penalty?"

"Because it's an election year, sweet Jo. He thinks he has enough evidence for a jury to believe that Ed somehow lay in wait for a woman in her undies. He thinks the fact Ed was in their home, where she had a court order prohibiting him from being, is enough. The crazy thing about it is that maybe it is. A jury gets mad enough they just might recommend the death penalty."

"And you've got a client who wants to die," she said. "Won't Ed learn enough about the facts during the trial, find out enough about what Herman wants, so that when he goes on the stand he can supply the need?"

"Maybe," I said, smiling a little. "If I put him on."

"I thought he had a right to testify?"

"Right. And if I don't let him testify he might use it in a later appeal, but it would be an appeal to reverse his conviction. I'm thinking, if things go on as they are, that I'll call what witnesses we have, minus Ed, then rest. If he wants to testify I'll let him testify in the insanity part of the trial."

"That sounds tricky," she said dubiously.

"It is tricky."

"If you could make a deal for a term of years, would Ed go for it now?"

"He was willing enough before," I said. "After his pills didn't work I think he believed prison would kill him quick. His words, not mine. Now, I don't know. He was better with me earlier, more reactive to what I said, more tuned in on the world around him, more of a planner. I think when he woke up he was surprised to be alive. Now he seems barely on the planet." I shrugged. "But Doc Tyne says he's sane enough now so I'm stuck. I've got to go ahead. And my defenses of insanity at the time Beth died and intoxication just aren't much good where the prosecution can show the jury a dead body."

"All right," she said. "So you're going to try to find this book? Then what will you do?"

"Read it. Make some calls from the office after I read it. Maybe even see some people."

"And then?"

"What did you have in mind?" I asked, seeing she was smiling.

"The yard needs cutting."

"The golf course also needs us," I said. "First the grass, then golf?"

"Okay," she agreed.

The phone rang again. I went to it and watched it ring, undecided whether to pick it up or pull out the jack. I picked it up. It was a mistake.

The voice was muffled. "Mess this town up and keep doing what you're doing and I'll slice you, your pretty wife, and your brat into bloody bits."

I hung the phone up and unjacked it. The call worried me, but only a little. I'd had them before. The world is full of anonymous cowards. They write you unsigned letters and make threatening calls.

But now I had Joe and Jo to worry about.

CHAPTER FOUR

Rules of Procedure 14A: Discovery: To comply fully with the rules regarding discovery both plaintiff (state) and defendant must, when new witnesses are found after the final date for the exchange of information, immediately provide the other side with the names of witnesses, copies of documents, and where possible, what these new matters are likely to prove.

I got the key to the house from the realtor who'd listed it. I drove there, parked, and entered the big front door. I went over her bedroom first, but there was nothing. No one had been in to clean up the house or remove her things. There were soiled clothes in her hamper, panties and stockings, bras, and little peek-a-boo shirts of the kind she favored and liked to wear with the top buttons undone. The hamper smelled of mold and mildew and faintly of Beth's remembered perfume. She'd been a tease and a game player, but she'd also been a lot of woman.

When I didn't find the book in her bedroom in the stack of crossword puzzle books there I almost lost heart, but I kept on looking. It seemed to me, as I searched the house, that things were more jumbled than they should be. Clothes had been scrambled about in her drawers and some hangered things in her closet lay on the floor gathering dust. I wondered if someone else had been in after the police, someone looking for what I now sought and maybe finding it.

I went downstairs after a frustrating while and sat on a couch that had been covered by a sheet. Maybe I could go to the jail and ask Ed where she might hide things. Maybe I could go out to the farm and ask Ed Jr. Somehow I doubted they'd know. Ed Jr. would already have told me. Ed just wouldn't know.

An old house burglar I'd once represented in a divorce after he'd "retired" told me how he did houses. He said he walked through them and looked for things out of the ordinary, things that seemed out of place. I tried using his method. I walked again through the hot, silent house, looking here, looking there.

In the family room some books seemed out farther than others on disorderly shelves. I pulled out more crossword books and puzzle books that were out of line and discovered an alcove behind. I found the diary. I stood looking at it, heart racing, but not completely satisfied. I wondered if anyone else had seen it, read it, then replaced it. The pages were unnumbered and they were in spiral form. Someone could easily have removed a page or pages.

It wasn't all I'd hoped for, but it was far better than anything I had. It wasn't even a true diary in the sense that it followed Beth along day by day. What she'd done in keeping it was take one lined page for each man. She didn't have a date she'd started it listed, but there were dates in it. I wasn't in it so she'd not been keeping it at Beth and Robak time, now three-plus years back.

I went through it. There were only eight pages that had been used. They weren't numbered so there could have been more. Three of the names I already knew. One was an often-married car dealer who was perpetually chasing, another a construction man who'd built most of the new, large apartment buildings and schools in Bington. I'd heard they were already beginning to fall down and that he'd made a lot of money and so had others.

The third name I already knew was the one that had most disheartened Herman Leaks, Tinker Clippage's name. Tink was a county commissioner, an all-around nice guy with a wife and six, count them, kids. I wondered, when I'd first heard about Tink, where he got the energy. He was one of the callers who'd left his name at the office for me to return his call. I supposed if I did call anyone I'd call Tink. He was hard to dislike.

Beth had listed a man on each of the eight pages. She'd given their physical characteristics, color of eyes, hair, estimated weight and height, and then added intimate details.

Juror Number One wasn't on the list and I wasn't on the list. Doc Tyne wasn't either, but then I'd not expected him to be.

Following the physical data there were a number of stars. You could get up to ten stars. Then she'd kept count. Four sticks, then a stick through to make five, and start a new stick row.

There were also three dates, day of the month and month, and year, for each man with three sticks. After three dates she stopped putting them down, which might mean something.

I had a sudden technical inspiration. Rather than passing one book to the jurors, why not make lots of copies? One for the prosecutor, twelve, no fourteen, for the jurors and alternate jurors, one for the judge, and a couple of extras.

I looked again in the alcove. She'd stuck a couple of crossword puzzle books in there plus a book on party games. I went through them, but found nothing. I lost interest.

There were two names I didn't recognize among those on the eight pages. I figured they had to be out-of-towners she'd met someplace. But I'd show them to Steinmetz for corroboration. Steinmetz knew about everyone.

The book, when the word leaked out, held the possibility of ruin for some. The first date in it, and I now figured them to be the dates she'd been with the men listed, was slightly less than two years back. There were breaks in time when she'd either not been going with anyone or not been recording it. The most glaring was from December of last year through the date of her death. She'd either lived pure or lived unrecorded.

Of the new names some surprised me. One that did was Andy Parklin's name. He was a lawyer who'd once been a deputy in Herman's office but who'd quit and gone out on his own a year or so back. Rumor had it Herman fed him personal-injury work for an under-the-table percentage of the recovery. Unethical, but possible. Andy was young, personable, and recently married. There was also Sid Gellheiser, a widowed banker who was a frequent and heavy contributor to Herman Leaks's party finances. Sid was getting on in years, but he was a health nut, ramrod straight, and a big man at the local Baptist church. Best, or worst, of all was a listing for Bington's handsome, athletic mayor, Ferd Hoover. The whole town theorized he had to be a womanizer, but he'd never been caught good at it. He was married into Sid Gellheiser's sister's family, which meant much money. I wondered if Ferd and Sid knew about each other. Beth gave Ferd nine stars, almost her highest accolade.

One of the unknowns had ten stars. She'd made his twelve sticks in great, huge marks, as if to put the rest to shame. The name in the book was George Pitchford. It meant nothing to me. I wondered how and where she'd met him and then managed to meet him again that many times. She'd not listed his physical characteristics. Their trysts had begun in early October and the last date of the three had been about half through November. Then there were nine more marks. His final date was the last date in the book.

Maybe Steinmetz would know who George Pitchford was.

I put the "diary" in my jacket and took it to the office. Inside our Saturday-silent and stuffy building I made the obligatory call to the prosecutor's office. Since it was Saturday, Leaks's office was, of course, closed, but I wanted to be able to say or testify truthfully in court that I'd called Leaks as soon as possible after discovery of Beth's diary. Herman had an unlisted phone at home and its number was jealously guarded and kept from those of us who might dare to bother him on weekends. I didn't really blame him for that. I did about the same thing by unplugging my phone.

I thumbed through my file on the Sager case and found the lengthy witness list I'd supplied the prosecutor with back down the line at discovery time. Part of the legal game is listing everyone you can think of, everyone who knows anything about anything, and so frustrating the prosecutor into not taking depositions through his sheer awe at the size of your list. It had partially worked. Leaks had deposed Doc Tyne, Giles Sager, and Ed Jr. Then he'd quit.

These are supposed, by the rules, to be the days of "no surprise" trials, but many things still happen. Once I'd known we were going to trial I'd put in a few clinkers I hoped Herman would stumble over.

I placed the witness list on top of the file to remind me to update it with a supplement Monday morning.

I hid Beth's book in an old, rusting, long-closed file cabinet in the office filing room. I'd put a secretary to work on it Monday morning also. When she finished we could have a bit of new "show and tell."

I felt vaguely sorry about the new local men on the list. I knew them all and I wondered how long they'd sweated it out. They must now believe they were safe.

I'd have Sam King serve them Monday with subpoenas. Sam was large, pleasant, and built like a wedge. People tended to smile at Sam even when they were angry at him.

I sat down at my cluttered desk. There were case files flagged for me to look over, but nothing was critical yet. There were also letters and a stack of unread advance sheets. There was a stack of pink phone messages.

I called Doc Tyne. He answered the phone after half a dozen rings. His voice was sleepy and uncertain.

"I found Beth's diary," I said.

"Good for you," he said unenthusiastically.

"There are some names in it that could help us."

"Help Ed and you, not me," he said severely. "I'm only a witness for you. I'm not involved in Ed's cause."

"You want to see him get off, don't you?"

"Yes. I want him to get off because he was insane when he shot her."

"Okay," I said. "Tell me if Beth ever mentioned any of these names to you?" I read off the names in the book to him.

"I suppose so. They all sound familiar. Some of them I never heard of before Beth mentioned them. Like that last one you read, George Pitchford."

"She rated men. He got her highest rating."

"Now and then she'd go peeling off into some nearby city for a weekend. She'd get a hotel room and find someplace friendly. Maybe he was someone there."

"He spent a lot of time with her and she was impressed." I dug out a calendar from the desk drawer. "There are three dates listed for him. Two of them weren't weekends." I thought about that for a moment. It was puzzling.

He yawned audibly. "I've got to get some sleep." I thought I heard another voice in the background, muted, female laughter.

"Sure," I said. "Get some sleep." I hung up.

I looked down at the list of phone messages on their pink sheets, considering them. I figured I owed a call to one man at least. I called Tinker Clippage.

"Tink," I said, when he came on. "This is Don Robak. They said in the office you'd called."

"Sure I called. I've tried to call you at home, but there's never an answer," he said. "You sent some football type who claimed he was a legal eagle to serve me with some papers that don't make sense to me. I just put things back together with dear old Doris and then find you're hauling me into court on your problems."

"Could be your problem too," I said. "We have info you were seeing the late Mrs. Sager."

"Wrong, wrong," he said. "That's wrong. I knew her, but I wasn't one of her closer admirers."

"That's not the way it came to us. If you want to come in and say it was that way in court then come ahead."

"Don, baby, I don't want to come to court at all. This here's an election year and I'm up. I had a primary fight already. You drag me into court and kick some murder dirt on me it could be lots of folks who'd vote for me might change their minds. I don't want that. I want off the hook." He was silent a long moment and I was also. I remembered nights of kicking around the town and the nearby horse tracks with him long before my marriage, bright lights, bourbon on the rocks, and girls. He'd preceded Doc Tyne as a running partner.

"I want you not to call me as a witness," he said.

"Can't do that, Tink. I'm defending a man your old pal Herman Leaks has charged with murder. Herman wants the death penalty."

"He won't get that. You know it."

"Maybe, but you're one of the things I've got to fight him with."

"Not me," he said. His voice took on an edge. "There's a lot of boys out working on the county roads whose jobs depend on me. The word got out to them I'd been subpoenaed and they're worried about me. Some of them boys are rough, Don." He laughed. "You know the kind I mean, keep rocks in their shoes and catch their own bears. One of them might take it into his head to come after you. I'd sure not want that."

"Me too."

"I just want you to cool it, Don. We're friends and all of a sudden you're boxing me in with your problems."

"Sorry, Tink. It's the way it works." I thought about something. "You ever hear about Beth going around with a George Pitchford?"

"Never heard that name before," he said. "Are you saying I have to appear?"

"For now I'd say yes. Maybe something will work out, but there's nothing yet. Talk to Herman."

"I swear I've talked to him, Don. I've talked till my teeth turned blue. He's running and his problems are worse than mine. They say he'll climb over Ed's body to make his point." He was silent for a moment. "Maybe I just ought to go off on vacation?" His voice was questioning.

"If you do a lot of people will be looking for you. And the trial would stop until you got back. That isn't the answer, Tink. Maybe it would help if you checked around about who this George Pitchford was."

"I'll maybe ask around," he said. I could tell he was unhappy. He was used to getting his own way. "Meanwhile, I'd watch close if I was you. I hear people talking mean about you, Don. You get into these things and you turn them into circuses every time."

"If you give me a problem, Tink, then I'll give you a worse one."

"Doris will kill me," he said plaintively and hung up.

I sat awhile longer at my desk thinking about things. I was fairly sure, on a Saturday morning, where Mayor Ferd Hoover would be. There's a coffee club that meets in a downtown restaurant six days a week and Ferd was a member of the club.

I walked the two blocks to the restaurant and found him. He was seated at a big round table. There were twelve chairs around the table. It was Saturday, but the chairs were full.

"The legal beagle," someone yelled when I came through the door. The sun outside was bright and I was blinded by it a bit. I walked on back.

"All rise," said Jake Whitehead, who ran the local paper. He leaned forward. "When's the judge going to let you and Herm start talking again?"

"Soon," I said. "You know there's a jury and we start Monday?"

He nodded. "We're covering it."

Ferd Hoover sat nonchalantly in his chair watching me.

"See you privately a moment, Ferd?"

His eyes narrowed. "Little old me?"

"Yep. Little old you."

We weren't close, but we weren't enemies. "Why not just drag up a chair and ask what you want?"

I ignored the invitation. "It has to do with a lady."

"Knowing what you're into and what you've been doing plus all the skeletons you've been rattling that would have to be Beth Sager. I vaguely knew her." He smiled impudently. "I've heard there was a time when you knew her better."

"My best information is you knew her in the same fashion," I said evenly.

"Your information's incorrect."

I shrugged. "Fair enough. Let me ask you one more thing. Did you ever hear anything about anyone named George Pitchford?" I tried to think of the other out-of-town name, but it deserted me. Besides, Pitchford was the only recent one.

He shook his head. "No."

"Thanks," I said. I looked around the circle of heads at the table and gave them a quick, tight nod. "Nice to see you all." I looked back at Ferd and smiled. "See you in court, Ferd."

"What's that supposed to mean?" he asked.

I turned my back on him and headed for the door.

From the restaurant I walked back to the car. I drove home and cut grass. Later, in the middle of a muggy July afternoon, Jo beat me on the golf course. I had to give her a stroke a hole, but she'd have about beat me playing even. When we got home there were three anonymous letters in the mailbox. Two of them were vaguely threatening. The third wanted me to seek Jesus.

Sunday I visited Giles Sager and Ed Sager, Jr.

Giles was a farmer with a big place on the ridge. He was respected and he was good at the farming business. He grew about a thousand acres or so of soybeans and corn and a few acres of tobacco. He was horny-handed, powerful, slope-shouldered, and soft of speech. He spoke slowly and seemed to think over every word before he uttered it. I'd known him for a lot of years and liked him a lot. His wife was also a friend. She'd called Jo the day after Jo came home from the hospital with our son. They'd set a time, and then Mary had come to our house for a full day. She'd taught Jo a dozen things that day, things that made it easier for a woman with a new, first baby, things Jo hadn't known.

Once, years back now, a little group of schemers had roped Giles and Mary into a land scam. I'd extricated them from it. It had been a deal where the several promoters had made lengthy oral promises to Giles and a couple of his ridge neighbors about a ski resort. Much of it was to be located in the farm-useless hills on Giles's land, which lay along Hen Ridge, far above the river. The papers finally presented had been voluminous. Giles hadn't read them carefully. He'd had no lawyer read them for him. The promoters had mesmerized Giles and the others with big-dollar dreams. There'd been some very good up-front money paid Giles by the promoters. There'd been a sheaf of colorful stock certificates. There'd been a "time is of the essence" sense to the scam, with bright, apparently moneyed people breathing down the land owners' necks, another imaginary ski resort in the planning stage if this one didn't immediately finalize. It had been a first-class job done by con experts.

I'd dug my way suspiciously and laboriously into the background of the scammers when they filed their lawsuit against Giles and the others. Clauses unread in the long, involved contracts gave the scammers the right to purchase more land and they'd served Giles and the others notice they were exercising that option at about a third of what the added rich farmland was worth.

I'd tracked them and found them out. They'd tried to bribe me. When that hadn't worked they'd threatened me. When I ignored the threats and dug further I'd found the two head men had both served short time for other land swindles. They'd taken new names, but I'd found witnesses who'd angrily and positively identified them. Their financial and legal support buckled when I began asking knowledgeable deposition questions and failed entirely when I presented my witness list. No one showed from their side on the day of trial. An uncomplicated cross-action to quiet title put all things right.

Giles had about a thousand-plus acres. Most of it, except for the hill "ski" area, at the top of Hen Ridge, was prime farmland. I did his taxes for him every year. He never seemed to make a lot of money, but like a lot of farmers, he lived well. He spent January and February in Florida and then ten months on the land. He drove a Mojeff County Cadillac, more accurately described as a Ford pickup truck. He owed no one and there was money in the bank. He bargained hard for everything. He'd even bargained with me when he'd asked me to represent his brother.

"I know you and Ed ain't so close as you was years ago, Don, but what would it take in actual dollars to get you to defend him when his trial comes up?"

I'd smiled and named an outrageous figure.

"That much?"

"It's his life they want, Giles."

"Sure, but that's a hell of a lot of money too. The boy's got to be took care of. He'll get only what he gets from Ed. He's not Beth's." He nodded. "He can stay with me, but there's his school." He shook his head. "With the shape Ed was in I couldn't pay you that much. It just ain't there."

We'd limped to an agreement.

I knocked on the door and Mary Sager came and smiled at me.

"Giles and Ed are down back of the big barn," she said.

I walked on back.

It was a fine barn, well kept, old, but coated with new paint. Cattle watched me unblinkingly with bovine disinterest from the other side of their fence.

I found Giles and young Ed Jr. pitching horseshoes behind the barn.

"I thought you told me there was always work to do on the farm, Giles," I said.

Giles grinned. "I'm teaching Ed the finer points of this here game. Besides, it's Sunday."

I turned to Ed Jr. He was tall and still a little awkward, but like many today kids he'd inherited the best from his two parents, Ed and his long-deceased wife, Barb. He had a good smile and he'd lost ten or fifteen pounds of snack fat since he'd moved to the country and Giles's farm. He'd not gotten on well with either his stepmother or his father after the marriage. Once or twice, at Giles's request, I'd had to dig him out of juvenile problems and school truancies. He was so handsome he was almost pretty, but the farm had now toughened him and pared him down so that he looked much more boy than girl. He was a kid who'd needed roots and strong hands. He'd found them with Giles and Mary.

Giles's kids were gone from the home. Keck, the son and oldest, had married last year and did something for Purdue University that seemed to excite Giles and Mary. Edith, the daughter, had married an accountant three years back, someone she'd met at Hanover College. She lived five hundred miles from Bington.

"We start trial tomorrow," I said. "I'd like both of you to be around. I'm sure the prosecutor will ask for a separation of witnesses. He always does. If he doesn't this time, I will. But I'd like to have some witnesses standing up in court when the judge swears in those present. Maybe it'll make Ed feel better." I shook my head, not knowing.

Giles looked at Ed Jr. He nodded. "We'll be there, Don," Giles said. "I still can't figure out how we can be of much help in it. We both saw the things Beth was doing and watched Ed trying to drink hisself to death, but there's a God's plenty who saw the same. You showed me your witness list and told me what you wanted to do, but do you need it done so many times?"

"Now more than before," I said. "I found a kind of diary of Beth's and I'm adding some more names to the list of witnesses. If you could watch the whole trial, which you can't under a separation, you'd see Herman Leaks prove his case over and over. He'll introduce every statement, call every peace or police officer who was in the investigation, and everyone else he can. He'll call people who saw arguments between Beth and Ed. It won't make any difference to him or to judge or jury that the evidence is cumulative. That's the way a trial's done. When it's my time I intend to prove Ed's situation the same way. So I'll want both of you to testify about men visitors, her trips away from home, and Ed's drinking and money problems."

"Speaking of money, do you need any more yet?" Giles asked.

He'd given me some up front and I knew what had been paid so far was coming from him, not Ed. Ed might eventually be liquid, but his assets were frozen now.

"Not yet," I said. I'd have taken more money if he pressed me, but it seemed righter to wait and see what I could get from Ed.

Behind the place where they pitched horseshoes corn rose waist high against the hot, blue July sky. A line separated the corn to my left. There I could see a smaller patch of tobacco, then a large field of soybeans. No weeds and the lines of separation were sharp and clean.

"Looks like a good year," I said.

Ed Jr. gave the sky a practiced look, which I figured he'd learned from Giles. "We were thinking we could sure use a good, soaking rain before too long."

"Sure," I said, not smiling, but wanting to. The weather's never perfect on a farm. I've never met a farmer who'll admit to it being better than "fair."

CHAPTER FIVE

Procedure: The order of a jury trial shall be as follows: First, the court shall preliminarily instruct the jury, then the state shall, and the defendant may make opening statements.

Monday morning, a little past nine, Judge Harner read his brief preliminary instructions, starting with the indictment charging Ed, then the statute defining what various activities could constitute capital murder. He'd added to that instruction that there were lesser, included offenses. He then read other short instructions on burden of proof, presumption of innocence, and credibility of witnesses.

The courtroom was cool in the early morning and most of the jury was bright-eyed and alert. One lone juror, the laid-off factory worker, sat hunched down, his eyes almost closed. When he began to snore the sweet young English teacher next to him shook him awake.

Judge Harner finished his instructions just as the clock in the courthouse tower struck the half hour. Steinmetz had once confided to me that things were weakening where the huge clock was seated and that one day, probably in a storm, the whole thing might fall through. That seemed something to look forward to.

Herman Leaks sprang up quickly to make his opening statement. He pranced excitedly about the courtroom for a full hour. As I watched him I remembered what Steinmetz, when he was judge, had said about Herman: "He springs up like weeds near an outhouse."

Herman now had two deputies with him. Predictably he drew up an extra, empty chair at his counsel table. He did it with a flourish.

He went through the contents of the grand jury indictment pointing out how he'd prove the elements of the crime. He detailed what his evidence would show against Ed. Ed had "hidden" himself in the house he'd been ordered from and waited for Beth so as to kill her. Herman pointed vengefully at Ed, who sat bemused, watching, his face expressionless.

"That's the man who used his killer's gun and sprang out of hiding and shot his wife. That's Ed Sager, who broke God's law and man's law." He stopped and looked penetratingly at the jury and saw he had them all listening. He pointed to the empty chair. He lowered his voice. "There's one witness in this case you can't and won't hear testimony from. You'll see pictures of her and witnesses will tell you about her, but she won't be with us in the days that follow because she's dead. She should be sitting in this empty chair, but when the trial begins Sheriff Dorsett will be there instead. Beth Sager's in her grave. She cries out to you as jurors from there."

"Objections," I said. I cupped a hand to my right ear. "Has my hearing gone bad?"

"Sustained," Judge Harner said. "The jury will disregard the prosecutor's statements about someone calling to them from the grave."

Leaks nodded solemnly, unabashed. He took one more hack at the jury. "Remember the empty chair," he said hoarsely. He sat down and stared over at me triumphantly. He was a man who had great belief in his courtroom abilities and he could be fairly effective.

Earlier, in my office, I'd left one of the secretaries making copies of Beth's diary and typing up the new witness list. I expected her momentarily. I looked up at Judge Harner.

"Could I request a short break, your honor?"

He looked at his watch. It was now past midmorning and time for a break anyhow, so he nodded.

He admonished the jury about discussing or determining the case and sent them to the jury room. I went out into the hall and looked both ways, but there was no secretary. I went into the judge's outer chambers to call.

One of our office secretaries came bustling to the door as I was dialing so I rehung the phone. She had all the diary copies in a box with new witness lists stacked neatly on top. I filed the new witness list with the file stamp on the bench and gave a copy to Judge

Harner. He inspected it and raised his eyebrows. I put a copy of the list on Herman's counsel table. I also put a copy of the diary there. When the court reporter returned to the courtroom I had her mark the original as an exhibit.

"What's this now?" Leaks asked sharply, coming back and finding new things on his table. He handed the list of witnesses and the diary to a deputy.

I picked up my copies and examined them gravely. "It looks to me like an addition to the witness list I previously furnished you plus an exhibit I plan to offer in evidence, Herman. What's it look like to you?"

"Robak's playing games again, your honor," Leaks said, glaring at me. "Here we are into the opening day of trial and suddenly he wants to add to his list of witnesses." He shook his head. "Have the new ones been subpoenaed?"

"That's taking place now," I said. I'd given a copy of the old list to Steinmetz with the new names penciled in and he'd promised to have Sam King serve them.

"Tell the court why you waited until now to give me this stuff and add new witness names?"

I nodded at the judge. "I discovered these new names and this exhibit over this past weekend, your honor. I tried to call Mr. Leaks, but his office phone didn't answer. His home phone is unlisted. I've tried to get him before at his home without success. No one will give out the number. I therefore didn't have his home phone number to call him. Today, when my secretary brought over the new list and the exhibit, was my first chance to share them with the prosecution." I smiled over at Herman, who was now belatedly reading the names of the new witnesses. I watched his face lose color. "If the court wants to swear me I'll repeat under oath what I'm saying now."

Harner shook his head. "Not unless the prosecutor presses for it. Do you want Mr. Robak sworn, Mr. Leaks?"

"Some of these new people Mr. Robak plans to call are beyond reproach, your honor," Herman said obliquely and desperately. "Robak wants to turn this simple trial into a sex circus."

Judge Harner looked down at the list. "That could well be so, Mr.

Leaks. Did you want a continuance to depose any of the new witnesses?"

"Before I decide whether to do that might I have a few moments
to talk with Mr. Robak in private?"

"I'd rather not engage in any private discussions, Herman," I said
mildly. "Say what you want to say in front of the court."

"You're damned determined to turn this trial into some sort of
public sex show, aren't you, Robak?" Leaks accused hotly.

I shook my head. "The list is people who were close to the deceased. I merely want the jury to see how close. You claim my client
lay in wait and shot his wife in a cold, premeditated murder. My list
of witnesses, or some of them, will show what his reasons were for
his actions, that he might have killed her, if he did, in sudden heat.
They'll further show how her illicit behavior might have caused his
temporary insanity on the day of the crime."

"People like you are the reason why this state changed the law on
insanity," Leaks said.

"Which takes effect next year, Herman." I smiled at him. "You
decided to turn a routine husband killing wife into a capital crime."
I nodded. "I understand, Herman. After all, it's an election year and
we all know anything goes in an election year."

Leaks's face had gone from red to gray. "We should discuss this
out of the court's presence, Robak."

I shook my head. "No way, Herman. The last time I tried anything in this case with you in private I wound up with the state's
offer withdrawn."

In the front row of benches behind the railing which separated
the jury from the spectators a reporter from the Bington *Chronicle*
scribbled furiously. Leaks saw him.

"I never agreed to anything," he said, his voice lower.

"That's incorrect. You never signed any agreement, but then I
didn't expect you to once there was heat. After all, I've dealt with
you before. In this transaction you lived up to your reputation with
the bar."

Herman shuffled the papers I'd given him. I could see him twisting and turning inside himself. My insults were nothing to him, but

the new witness names were. He moved close to me and lowered his voice so the reporter couldn't hear.

"Would your client go for twenty now? I could ask for a continuance now and let him sit over in jail. Then we could do him later?"

"After November?"

"After November. He'd get good time credit for his jail time."

"I'll ask. Is it a formal offer?"

"Not formal," he said.

"I'll ask my client, Herman. I don't think he'll go for it."

Outside the window the squirrels were playing tag again. Ed Sager sat watching them, oblivious to what was happening around him. His neck was red and slightly puffy, but there seemed to be no other signs of his weekend try at suicide. I explained the situation to him in whispers while the reporter tried to figure out what was going on.

"You mean I'd get sentenced to twenty years, but only have to serve ten at most and maybe be out in far less than that?" he asked.

"Keep your voice down," I said. "I've got a politician who wants to be reelected and who'll trade anything to do it. He's offered just what he offered before, with you to sit it out in jail, getting credit for the time, until after the election."

He thought for a long moment and then shook his head. "No, Don, I don't want that. I want to tell my story about that day and let the jury decide whether I live or die. I don't want anyone getting me out of what I guess I did."

I handed him the original copy of Beth's diary. "Look this over, Ed. See what Beth did to you, look who she did it with, how many times she hung new horns on you. Is a death you now don't even remember worth your taking a chance on your own life?"

He glanced incuriously at the book and then laid it down. "I guess it is to me. I don't expect you to understand. You're my lawyer and you're trying your best to help me. I know this and sometimes I even like it. Saturday it all got to me and I tried to hang myself and thought I'd gotten it done. I won't do that again, but I still want out of this world. I was afraid Saturday. I'm more afraid now. I've not got the courage to try Saturday again." He shook his head, his eyes sad and lost. "I can tell the story about Beth and me. Maybe the

jury will do it for me. You see, when it happened, I still loved her."
His eyes sought mine. "Do you understand me?"

"No," I said. And I didn't.

"Perhaps there ought to be someone else? You and I were close
friends once and now you want to save me and you keep working to
save me. Perhaps if it was someone else . . ."

"If you change lawyers now there'll be a continuance, Ed. Your
trial won't start today. A new lawyer would have to look over every
bit of your mess just as I've looked it over. And any lawyer worth a
fee will fight what Herman Leaks, with your help, is trying to do."

He nodded, perhaps understanding what I was saying even if I
didn't understand him. "I guess we're stuck together then, Don. Go
tell them I won't take their deal. Let's get the trial going."

"All right," I said. "For my protection I want to do it on the
record. I want to have it show I advised you to take the offer."

"Sure. Okay."

I shook my head. "You're a poor simpleton, Ed. Once that goes in
the record, and it's going to, I doubt any appellate court would let a
death sentence stand even if you fight to keep it."

He shrugged. The papers had been full recently of stories about a
mass killer who'd refused legal aid and had died in the electric chair.

"I'll take my chances and not their deal," he said.

I went back to the bench. Herman waited.

"Turn on the recorder and take this please," I said softly to the
court reporter.

She looked up at Judge Harner, who nodded assent.

"I told him of your possible offer, Herman. He refused to accept
it. I've advised him to accept it, but he won't." I turned to Ed.
"Come up here, Ed." I waited until he shambled up. "Isn't that
right, Mr. Sager? Didn't I tell you there was a good possibility, if
you'd plead out to an included offense to capital murder, that you'd
get a twenty-year sentence?"

"Yes sir," he said. "I don't want to do it."

The frustrated newspaper reporter was at the edge of the railing
trying to hear and understand what was happening.

I smiled at Herman. "I guess we both get our circuses."

He shook his head in disbelief. "You're still going to call all those people?"

"Probably. Unless things change."

"Why? All you'd be doing is tearing down reputations, doing malicious damage."

"And presenting alternatives to the jury."

"Your honor," Leaks protested. "I'd ask the court to look over the additions to Robak's witness list. There are people in it who are in sensitive positions. Robak only wants them here to cloud the issue."

"Their names are in her diary," I said. "I want to ask them why. I want them to explain why they're in her diary and what her remarks in the diary mean."

Judge Harner sat stiffly. "I can't control what witnesses Mr. Robak calls, Mr. Leaks." His voice was indecisive.

"You can control what's germane to this trial. All Robak plans to do is try Beth Sager instead of Ed Sager. That's all right, but some of the people he'll use are in business. One's even a local lawyer who practices in this court. Another's a banker. Several hold high political office."

"The names are in her diary," I said again.

"How do we know it's her diary?" Leaks asked, seeing a new opening.

"If I can't get it identified then you can object to its admission when I offer it."

Judge Harner nodded. I didn't think he liked the list of witnesses either, but he could be a statesman. He didn't run again for four years.

"I'll grant you a short continuance if you desire it, Mr. Leaks," he said.

Herman shook his head like a dog coming up out of deep water. "No, I guess not." One of his deputies pulled urgently at his shoulder, but Leaks shook him off. "We'll go on."

The judge nodded to the bailiff. "So be it. Let's get back to business. Bring the jury in."

The jurors struggled into their chairs. Later, as they made more trips in and out of the jury room, they'd get it down to a routine where goings and comings would work like a good clock, but now they were awkward about it. We waited them out.

I went to the lectern. Judge Steinmetz and other good lawyers before him had taught me not to oversell. I talked reasonably to the jury about insanity. I read them the law pertaining thereto from notes I'd made. I told them they'd hear a lot of evidence about the lives of both Beth and Ed Sager. I told them briefly about what an intoxication defense consisted of and read them an instruction I intended to submit as a final instruction.

"We'd also like to have Beth Sager here today," I said, pointing to the empty chair. "If she were here she might tell us what happened before and on the day she met her death. That's not possible, but we'll do our best to reconstruct some of those times for you. There will, of course, be so-called confessions. Those confessions are really only statements, conflicting in nature, made by Ed Sager in his grief and despair after his wife's death. I'd like to ask you to please listen to every word of every statement. Try to find out from them, if you can, what happened to Beth Sager on the day she died four-plus months back. You'll find there's not much to those statements except words spoken by a police or peace officer and answered in the affirmative by Ed Sager. In other words what you'll hear will be phrases put in Ed Sager's mouth by officers who thought they knew the facts surrounding Beth's death. They differ. Maybe if Beth were here she could tell us the true story."

I had them listening now so I walked to the empty chair and stared down at it for a long, silent moment, waiting until the jury grew restive in their chairs.

I counted lawyers loudly. "One, two, three lawyers it needs to present the state's evidence. At first I thought this empty chair might be for one more state's prosecutor."

Leaks gave me a scornful look, but a couple of the jurors smiled.

"All this legal firepower gathered together by the state has me so shook up I've not been sleeping well nights. As a result I've asked one of my law partners, a former judge of this court, Mr. Steinmetz, to come over and protect me from the state's wrath. He'll be in and out during the course of the trial starting tomorrow."

I appealed to them. "All the defense in this case asks is that each of you listen to it all from beginning to end. Don't make up your minds until you've heard everything. I'd like for you to give special attention to our psychiatrist, Dr. William Tyne, who had both Beth Sager and Ed Sager as patients. If, when the trial is done, you believe Ed Sager killed his wife then try to figure out the 'why' of it. Did he intend to do it? Did she drive him to it? What made him do it? Was he insane when he did it or was he so intoxicated he could not have formed the intent to do it? If you listen to our evidence carefully you'll hear how Beth Sager drove her husband to alcoholism and from there into the misty outer realms of madness and how her salacious conduct put him in a pressure cooker which became his life. That pressure cooker may have eventually exploded, but Ed Sager doesn't know it even now. He remembers very little of that final day for Beth. All he's sure about is finding her body, then taking up the little gun which killed her, and trying to kill himself, a project he still seems bent on accomplishing." I held up my hands to them. "Listen to this case with both your hearts and your heads. The judge will explain the law to you at conclusion, but you must hear and determine the facts. Some things won't be pleasant, but please see and listen to it all."

I sat down.

"Preliminary motions, gentlemen?" Judge Harner asked.

Leaks scurried to the bench. He then came to my table and dropped a copy of a motion in *limine*. It asked the court not to allow me to introduce evidence of the deceased's unfaithfulness except at those times near or around the date of her death. Leaks smiled over at me as I read it.

"I'll move the court orally for a separation of witnesses," I said.

"Show motion for separation of witnesses granted," Judge Harner said. "Then show the prosecution's motion in *limine* overruled."

"I'd like to argue on that out of the presence of the jury," Leaks said, his face reddening again.

Judge Harner contemplated him and I realized that my greatest ally in this case might be the judge. Steinmetz had told me it didn't take any judge long to wear himself out on Herman Leaks.

"Why bother?" The judge's voice was mild, but unwavering. "It's discretionary and you know it, Mr. Leaks." He nodded and said, "Come up now, both of you."

We went up to the bench.

Harner's voice was low, only loud enough for the two of us to hear.

"There's a man on trial for his life here and you want the jury not to know his reasons for doing what he did if they don't fit into a time frame you consider convenient." He smiled. "That's assuming the defendant did anything at all. Again, the motion is overruled." He looked up at the wall clock. "It's almost noon. We'll break now, send the jury on to lunch, and come back fresh to the battle at one-thirty."

CHAPTER SIX

Ann. Statutes: A person who knowingly kills another human being commits murder, a felony.

We reconvened at the appointed hour and Leaks called his first witness. That witness was, predictably enough, the sheriff of Mojeff County, Abraham (Abe) Dorsett. He was an ex-state police detective and the first sheriff Mojeff County had elected in my years there with actual police training. Most of the tenants of that venerable office, back the line, had been better politicians than police officers, but Abe was good in both areas. I doubted his opponent, from my party, would get within rifle shot of him come the fall election. Abe, like all wise politicians, didn't believe it and spent much of his available time plotting against the forbidding future. He'd asked me to vote for him at least half a dozen times and I'd assured him, each time, I would. He was a big, quiet man with good sense, some humor, and a knack for getting along with the world. He ran his office well. He was now in his far fifties, a hunter, a fisherman, a teller of jokes, and the perpetrator of a hundred sly tricks on his deputies, the lawyers who came in and out of his office, and fellow office holders. He drank sour mash whiskey in moderate amounts and smoked black, acrid cigars. I like him.

He took the oath along with a number of others, including Ed Sager, Ed Sager, Jr., Giles, and others in the courtroom. One other of my defense witnesses was there. He was an old friend and a recent drinking acquaintance of Ed Sager's: Wade "Preacher" Smyth. I planned to use him as a witness to Ed's drinking habits.

The judge then excused the witnesses, other than Sheriff Abe, from the courtroom. I winked at Ed Jr. and Giles as they departed and nodded at Preacher. They could go home now and await call.

I'd asked them to be there primarily because it made me a little less lonely. I hadn't asked Preacher, but he'd come. I was touched he'd done that for Ed or me. Testifying wasn't going to be easy for Preacher. I'd explained that to him weeks back, but he'd only nodded and smiled.

Abe climbed nervously into the witness chair. He crossed his ankles and then uncrossed them self-consciously. He smiled at the jury, the prosecutor, and the judge. He then included me, but his smile was wary.

He stated name and profession.

"How long have you been a police officer?" Leaks asked.

"More than thirty years."

"Tell the jury something about your background as a law officer."

I got to my feet. "Is the prosecution attempting to qualify Sheriff Dorsett as some kind of expert witness?"

"Is that an objection?"

"Not yet, your honor. I'll call it an inquiry."

"Inquire during cross-examination," Judge Harner advised.

Leaks smiled at me, hiding it from the jury. He was a very apparent lawyer. Early victories sometimes relaxed and lulled him.

"I used to be with the state police. I retired from being a state officer the year before I became sheriff. For my last eight years with the state police I was a detective."

"Did you investigate many homicides?"

"Yes. I counted up once a few years back and it was then about forty. There've been a few more since, maybe five or six."

"Were you the duly elected and acting sheriff of Mojeff County on the nineteenth of March of this year?"

"I was."

"In regard to the case we're presently trying, what happened on that day?"

"Well, first off we received an anonymous phone call. As a result we went out to the Sager place a mile or so out on River Road."

"What time did you receive the telephone call?"

"It was about three in the afternoon. I checked my log before I came over here today and it said we'd taken the call at one minute to three."

"The call came from whom?"

"Whoever it was wouldn't give us a name. I thought it was a man." He shook his head, unsure about it. "If it was a woman she had a deep voice."

"After the call you proceeded to the Sager house?"

"Yes. We took a patrol car and drove on out there."

"What time did you arrive on the scene?"

"Before three-fifteen. After three, of course."

"What exactly did you find?"

"The front door to the house was standing open. It was a medium-cold day, temperature in the low forties, so that was suspicious. After we parked in front and walked up the steps I could see some stockinged feet sticking out into where the hall opened into the big room where there was a wet bar and doors that opened to the swimming pool. It was very bright inside because the back wall of the room is mostly glass and the pool's in a patio behind the glass."

"The pool was empty?"

Abe nodded. "It was March."

"Whose feet did you see?"

"Beth Sager's. We yelled we were coming in and a voice yelled back to come on in. That was Ed."

"You were invited into the house by Ed Sager?"

"Yes."

"What did you see when you entered?"

"Beth Sager, Mr. Leaks. She was faceup and spread out on the floor. She had a wound in her forehead, right between her eyes. There was a larger, exit wound in the back of her head. I checked her pulse and felt her forehead and she was dead, and had been for a while. There was blood on the floor under her and the room was messed up, stuff broken on the floor, most of it glasses. There was a lamp turned over. Beth was wearing panties and a bra and I guess nylon stockings. There was a robe over a chair near her. Ed Sager was sitting up against the wall out to the pool. He had the .38 derringer. He was clicking it up against his head. He did it a couple of times before I got the gun away from him. He had a bottle of Jim

Beam beside him." Abe thought for a moment. "He kind of nodded at me when I took the gun from him. He said, 'Hi, Abe.'"

"Did he act out of the ordinary?"

"No. He acted normal to me. He'd been drinking some."

"Anyone else in the area of the house?"

"Not that we ever saw or heard about."

"Did you look around?"

"Yes. We searched the house and the grounds, but there wasn't anyone else around. No other cars around either. Just Ed's old Plymouth and Beth's Lincoln. And no other guns."

I nodded inwardly. I'd asked Ed about the things the sheriff was testifying about during one of his more receptive times. Ed told me he'd not seen anything or anyone or heard anything of interest. I had no reason to believe he was lying.

"After those first words Ed Sager said to you did he ever say anything else in that room where his wife had been shot?"

I got to my feet. "One moment, your honor. May I ask some preliminary questions?"

The judge nodded. "Proceed, Mr. Robak."

"Abe, before you started talking to Ed Sager did you read him his rights?"

"Sure, Don. I got me this plastic card the state give me and I carry it with me in my billfold. I've had it since way, way back when that Miranda business first began. Soon as I saw the way it was in the house and we got the gun from Ed I got out my card and read his rights to him."

"Read it to me again now," I said. "Read it to me exactly like you read it to him."

"Sure, Don." He hunted in his billfold, found the card, and read the standard Miranda warning.

"How intoxicated was Ed Sager at the time you read his Miranda rights to him?"

"He had some to drink for sure, but he kept wanting to talk about what had happened and about Beth. He kept saying he was sorry, real sorry. He was very rational about it once we got the gun."

"All right, Abe. What did he say to you when he'd had some to drink for sure?" I stole a quick look over at Leaks. One of his deputies was finally whispering to him, probably telling him I was stealing from his case.

"He said, 'I guess I killed her. I've been thinking about killing the little bitch for a long time.'"

"And he was intoxicated?"

"I guess like usual. Ed drinks a bit." He smiled without humor. "Or did."

"How much does he drink?"

"Objection," Leaks said. "I've been more than patient in this."

"Withdraw the question for now," I said. I sat down.

Leaks moved in on Abe again. "In your inspection of the house what did you find?"

"Well, the coats had all been pulled down in the front-hall closet."

"Pulled down?"

"Yes. Someone had pulled them all off their hangers and made a kind of nest of them back in one corner of the closet. There was an empty pint bottle of wine back there in the coats."

"What kind of wine?"

"Cheap stuff."

"Was there any other wine in the house?"

"No."

"Okay. After talking to him did you then take the defendant on to jail?"

"Yes," Abe said. "I arrested him. He's been in my jail ever since except when he's been over here for hearings or up at the mental hospital for tests." He moved restlessly in the witness chair and his belt and holster squeaked.

"Did he ever act abnormal in your jail? Throw any fits? Do anything out of the ordinary?"

"No. I guess he tried to kill himself once or twice, but he was pretty despondent about Beth."

Leaks nodded sagely for the jury and then led Dorsett through the evidence about how the crime scene had been closed, what had been done to protect and secure it, who appropriated the various items of evidence after they were collected, who had charge of the area police property room at the state police barracks. He asked Abe about what other officers were called in to assist in the investigation. I already knew the answers to the questions asked, but I listened. It was my job to listen. Later in the trial I knew I'd have a state ballistics expert to contend with.

All appeared routine. Sheriff Abe had made his run, found a body, found that body's husband in the same room, drinking heavily, holding the murder gun. Moreover, the accused was where he had no right to be, there having been a court order prohibiting him being in or about the house while the latest divorce action between Beth and Ed pended. I sighed inwardly while the sheriff told about serving that order and it was exhibited to the curious jury.

The case was a natural, a cinch.

"Did you talk more with the defendant after you took him into custody and placed him in jail?" Leaks asked.

"Sure. I'd go past his cell in the jail and he'd maybe nod to me like he wanted to talk. Ed and I'd known each other for a lot of years and I'd had him in the jail before for drinking offenses. I'd stop and he'd tell me again he'd killed her, but that he didn't remember it real well, but he was sure sorry about it now. I guess he did that maybe a dozen times."

"You weren't asking him questions?"

"No. He'd just volunteer the information, kind of blurt out things."

"You didn't read him a Miranda warning every time you walked past his cell?"

Abe Dorsett shook his ponderous head. "I figured Mr. Robak had told him about talking to us by then." He smiled over at me. "Ed had him a lawyer to tell him what to say and what not to say after he got to jail."

Juror Number One McNear laughed lightly and I saw a few other jurors grin.

"Move to strike the answer," I said, rising and sounding angrier about it than I was. I'd told Ed not to talk to anyone without me being present. It was something I told all clients accused of crime. In Ed's case it hadn't worked at all. He'd talked and talked. He'd talked to Abe Dorsett, to Abe's deputies, and even to prisoners who'd passed through the jail. He'd talked, even when I was present, to anyone who'd listen, to anyone he could do a *mea culpa* for. He'd confessed so many times that, taken all together, the confessions were a yawn. The state's problem wasn't one of paucity, but the confessions could be, and I intended would be, problems. The confessions had been made in front of many police officers. Each police officer had a slightly different version of the crime in mind as Ed was questioned. So there were many versions of Beth's death. Yes, he'd hid. Yes, he'd been angry at her. Sure, he'd been drinking, a little, a lot. No, she'd not attacked him, but yes, she had. Yes, she'd taken off her house coat to slow his anger, but no it had been off when he came out of his hiding place in the closet. He'd killed her and then walked by the river. He'd walked by the river, then killed her. . . .

"Motion granted," Judge Harner said. He leaned out toward Abe Dorsett. "Abe, you know better. The jury will totally disregard the sheriff's last answer."

Abe looked discomfited. Leaks smiled at the jury and then icily at me. Then patiently he started introducing written statements signed by Ed and witnessed by Abe. The method they'd first used with Ed was to tape the confessions, type them up from the tapes, then have Ed sign the typed version. Each time in the early days of Ed's tenure in jail they'd meticulously gone through the Miranda warning with him, both before and after I'd taken his case. Each time, even after I was in, he'd said he didn't want me or any other lawyer present, confessed again, then signed whatever the stenographer typed up.

All of it made for a lot of jury paper shuffling as copies were read by them so they could compare what Ed had said on tape with what Leaks's peerless stenos had made of it.

I endured in silence. Now and then Leaks would look over in my direction. *Got you this time, you bastard,* the looks would say. I thought he was right about that.

It was late afternoon before I got my chance. Leaks ran out of signed and witnessed confessions and turned Abe Dorsett over to me for cross.

I got up and walked to the side of the jury. I like for juries to watch witnesses while they testify, not watch me. Many lawyers, some of them good ones, like to get right in the face of a witness and confront him so their disbelief subtly becomes a part of the testimony. That can be effective when the witness has problems, but Abe had none I could think of to exploit.

"Sheriff, return with me now to the scene of the crime. You'd had some kind of anonymous call and that made you drive out to the Sager home?"

"Yes."

"How far is the Sager home from the closest neighboring house?"

"A ways. Maybe a hundred yards, maybe further. There's some houses down on the river. In March lots of them aren't occupied." He smiled. "This summer lots aren't either."

"How's that?" I asked.

He smiled some more. "It always cuts the traffic way down out there when someone shoots someone. I mean a lot of those river houses get used by people meeting people who they ain't married to."

"I see. That's fascinating, Sheriff. So Beth's death has had some effect on the number of love-ins in the neighborhood?"

Leaks was up. "Objection."

"Withdraw the question," I said quickly. The jury had heard it. I went back to what was at hand. "How far is the house from the city limits of Bington?"

"I clocked it. It's one point two miles."

"And how far back away from the River Road is the Sager home?"

"A couple of hundred yards. There's a road and a row of them tall, bendy trees that lead up the drive. And the house is a big place."

"Can you see the house from the River Road?"

"Sure. Or you could then, in March. I guess you could see it now through the trees."

"Could a passerby on the highway see what you saw on that day when you got to the Sager home?"

He blinked twice. "Maybe. I don't know."

"I mean the feet sticking out?"

He shook his head, seeing where I was heading. "No way. The

thing I figured out on it was that someone heard the sound of the gun and called us, or maybe he heard them fighting and arguing. Or maybe he just saw the door was ajar and called because of that."

"From a hundred yards away on the River Road?"

"Well, it's a pretty house, what you might refer to as a 'show place,'" he explained. "People drive out there to look at the river and some of them stop and look at the house. I've seen lots of cars parked off the road out there."

"Did you see anyone parked off the side of the road on the day of the shooting?"

"No."

"Did you ever get a report from anyone that they saw a car parked there that day?" I pursued.

"No, but someone sitting off the highway might have seen something or heard something. We got the call. That's a fact, so maybe someone did," he said reasonably.

"Okay, Sheriff. Tell the jury what the inside of the house looked like that day when you got there."

"There'd been an altercation of some kind. Ed didn't remember much about it. Some pieces of furniture were pushed over, small pieces, an end table, a light wicker chair. There was a broken table lamp on the floor. The room had a wet bar in it. Some of the glasses on the shelves behind it had been pushed off and broken." He nodded. "Might have made a lot of noise."

"Just exactly what did your anonymous caller say?" I asked, irritated a little. The sheriff was going to show the jury he was right about someone seeing or hearing something from the road.

"Objection," Leaks said, rising. "Hearsay."

"I'm asking the sheriff to relate what he heard on the office phone to send him out to where a shooting victim was discovered," I said. "It's close enough to the event to make it a part of the *res gestae*. He's already testified, on questioning by the prosecutor, that he did get a call and did go out to the Sager home."

Judge Harner hesitated. I thought he could rule either way without error.

"Witness may answer," he said.

Leaks sat down. He knew and I knew what had been said on the telephone and it was innocuous enough.

"The caller said something was badly wrong at the Sager home on River Road," Dorsett said.

"The caller identified the home by who lived there?"

"Yes."

"Was the voice cultured or uncultured?"

"I don't remember thinking on it one way or the other."

"Think now, Abe."

He shrugged, causing his leather parts to squeak again. "Cultured maybe." He shook his head. "I don't know."

"Did the caller say the Sager home or did he say the Beth Sager home?"

"He just said the Sager home. He used the exact words I'm using, as best I can remember."

"You took the call?"

"I took it."

"And it was enough to send you driving frantically out to the Sagers?"

"Sure. They'd had trouble out there before," the sheriff said, hurting my case a little, but not unexpectedly. "Ed, he wasn't supposed to be out there at all. I served him with his divorce papers right before Christmas and there was that restraining order with them."

"Had he violated previous court orders not to go there?"

"Sure, several times. She was forever filing divorces and then dismissing them."

"Okay. In the times he'd been out there before in violation of a restraining order had Ed ever harmed his wife?"

"No. I guess not. He'd broken stuff up before." Abe smiled his good smile at me and the jury, remembering. "Once, the summer before, he broke a bunch of drinking glasses and threw the pieces in the swimming pool. I guess he snuck in. Beth and a guest didn't know about the glass and they both got cut some trying to swim in the pool."

"What guest was that?" I asked innocently.

"Objection," Leaks said, bouncing to his feet. "Irrelevant without the time being established and some relation made as to what we're trying here."

I knew the day had been nine months-plus prior to Beth's death and that the swimmer who'd cut himself had moved on from Bington a few months thereafter. So I smiled and said, "Withdraw the question." The jury would hopefully wonder what Herman hadn't let them hear about and then, later, relate the question to other male visitors at Beth's house.

"To the best of your recollection, Sheriff Dorsett, and based on the reports from both the city of Bington and Mojeff County, which you have access to, had Ed Sager ever seriously injured his wife prior to March 19?"

"No, not that I ever knew about. That ain't to say they didn't fight, Don. Sometimes, when I'd get a call there, she might be a little bruised, but it would usually be on her wrists where he'd had to hold her off when she went for him."

I nodded as if surprised. "Oh? You mean that Beth attempted at times to assault Ed Sager?"

Abe Dorsett smiled. "Yes. She wasn't a big lady, but she was pretty healthy. And she liked to lay it on him when he was into the booze."

I could see Herman writhing a bit in his seat, wanting to object, but afraid to.

"Okay. Did you happen to check Ed on the day Beth died to see if he had any bruises?"

"I did and I didn't see any. I did see he was drinking, but he knew where he was and he seemed sane to me."

That hurt, but I pressed on. "You came in and the two of them were the only people around. Beth was dead and Ed was trying hard to shoot himself with a defective gun. Nevertheless, Ed was okay?"

"Sure, Don. He was clicking the gun against his head. It's one of them small derringers, a .38 caliber. They work by one chamber, in this case the top, going off and then when you pull the trigger again the bottom chamber's supposed to go. But the firing pin was bent in on the bottom chamber and wouldn't fire the shell in that barrel. The onliest way he could have made it work was take out the shell case in the top chamber and put the unfired shell from the lower barrel there. Then it would have worked. Ed was maybe too fried to think of that."

"By 'fried' do you mean intoxicated?"

"Yes."

"So you took the gun and then asked him about what had happened?"

"Yeah." He gave me a suspicious glance, perhaps thinking I was trying to trip him up. "I asked him after I'd read him his Mirandas. I asked him why he'd killed her. He mumbled something about being sorry and said he didn't know exactly what had happened."

"On a scale of one to ten, with one being low and ten being high, how drunk was Ed?"

He thought about it for a moment. "Maybe a five for Ed. About normal for him. I've seen him better. I've seen him passed out a few times too."

"And all he said was that he was sorry?"

Dorsett hesitated. "He kept mumbling about that."

"And you said he seemed okay mentally to you?"

"Same as always," he answered quickly.

"As a state trooper and as sheriff, how many people have you observed up close who eventually wound up being examined by psychiatrists?"

"Lots," he said, nodding. "I'd guess hundreds."

"Did your opinion as to the sanity or the insanity of those people always agree with that reached by the psychiatrists?"

He smiled. "No. Sometimes I'd think the subject was short in the head and psychiatrists would say they was okay. Sometimes I'd think they was okay and they'd get committed to the flyaways."

"Then you don't think yourself an expert?"

He gave me a look. "I'm pretty good at it. I don't miss often."

"Is Ed pretty despondent still about Beth?"

"Yes."

"Say again, so I can be sure, what cars were at the house."

"Well, Ed's old one. He didn't have no driver's license and he wasn't supposed to drive, but he did some anyway. Then Beth's Lincoln. It was in the garage."

I glanced over at Ed Sager. He'd slumped deep in his chair. He wasn't watching what was going on. I thought he might be asleep, but then I saw his eyes flicker.

I'd gotten a few things I wanted out of Abe Dorsett. I gave it up. "Your witness again," I said.

I saw the prosecution table confer about what I'd asked.

"No redirect," Herman said, after the conference.

He then called John Kissell, the deputy sheriff who'd made the run with Abe Dorsett. Kissell testified briefly. Herman then went to a state trooper who'd been called and taken possession of the gun which had killed Beth. Again, a short witness. After that there were two more state troopers who'd been briefly on the scene.

We were beginning to draw a crowd of spectators as word spread through downtown Bington that the trial was in progress. A robbery trial won't draw a crowd, thefts bring empty courtrooms, but murders still draw curious audiences in small towns like Bington. Those spectators came and went at peculiar times, rustling in and out of the courtroom, their empty seats soon filled by new faces. I recognized some faces, but most I didn't. At recesses they'd covey together in the halls, whispering and cackling. I hoped some of the whispers and cackles had to do with sweet Beth Sager.

At the end of a very long day I leaned tiredly back in my chair at the counsel table and looked up into the dark of the high ceiling above me. Herman Leaks had proved Beth Sager was dead, he had the gun found in Ed's hand in evidence, and the jury had heard half a dozen statements made to the various law-enforcement officers by Ed Sager. Leaks had exhibited Beth's blood-spotted brassiere to a curious jury and passed them some photos taken of the room and Beth's body.

It had been a productive day for the state.

Above me, where the ceiling of the courtroom turned from deep gray to almost black, I thought I heard the sound of wings. Birds nested up there. I'd seen them. One lawyer swore that a pigeon had landed on his counsel table during a bench trial, but he was a lawyer given to exaggeration and he drank a bit.

I gave the day to Herman by a wide margin, two birds at least.

A deputy sheriff came and stood politely by me for a time. I nodded at him finally and he started Ed on his trip back to jail. Ed went silently, not looking back at me, his eyes downcast. A small crowd of curious spectators waited at the door. They parted to let him and his convoy through.

A note in the office told me to join Judge Harold Steinmetz at the downtown Moose.

He was seated at a table. He had a drink in front of him and a copy of the diary I'd found in Beth's place.

I got a drink at the bar and joined him.

"Interesting reading? There were two people in there who must be from out of town," I said.

He held up one finger. "Just one. I can't place George Pitchford."

"How about Albert Stull?" He was the other name I'd not recognized in the book and he was an early entry.

"Bank examiner. Lived here in Bington, but spent most of his time on the road."

"Lived here?"

Steinmetz nodded. "He died maybe eight or nine months back. He died before Beth was killed. He was in a car accident over near the interstate and got himself killed."

"Well, that rules him out."

"What did Herman do when you served him his copy of this?" he asked.

"Made us a good offer, but Ed wouldn't take it."

"I see." Steinmetz raised his plastic glass. The bar had begun using plastics some months back, to the dismay of purists like Steinmetz and myself.

He peered into the depths. "I've gotten used to these plastic glasses and, these days, they kind of excite me."

"All right," I said, waiting.

"Sure. I've had so many operations. I've got a plastic vein in each leg and a plastic valve in my heart. My glasses and maybe my teeth are made of plastic. So this is the only place in town I can go to get excited unless I drive out past the plastics factory."

I grinned.

"That's better," he said. "Your face was long enough to fit in a milk bottle when you came in." He shook his head. "Why do we do it?"

"I guess because it's what we do," I answered simply.

"Okay," he said. "You want me tomorrow?"

"Yes," I said. He was the best man I'd ever seen in a courtroom and I wanted him.

One drink turned to two.

I went home finally. Jo let me eat a cold dinner in silence. I retired, wounded, to our screened porch and sat staring out into the failing light, which soon turned to darkness. I thought. Night birds called to each other with songs I didn't understand, but there were lots of things I didn't understand. There was a cool breeze.

Jo came once to the door and stared out at me, then gave me up as a bad job and retired inside to watch television with Joe beside her in his crib. After a while I could hear the soft burr of her snoring.

I went inside and looked at her as she slept. A good friend had told me that when I looked at her my eyes always seemed to get one shade lighter and that he'd seen us flirting, watching each other, and smiling across the room at crowded parties. I knew I wanted no one else.

Joe moved about in his crib and I saw his brown eyes were open. I moved close. I wasn't much yet for lifting him and holding him, but we did have one routine. I put my index finger near his hand and he closed perfect, tiny fingers around my larger finger. After a few moments his fingers loosened and I saw he was asleep again.

In a year or two I'd get him a bat and ball and maybe a train set. Then some running shoes. In a few more I'd teach him all I knew about jury trials. That ought to take all of a day. I thought about age and youth. Life's short. I was still trying to figure it out.

I went back to the porch and sank into my chair.

I heard something outside, something which cut into my thoughts.

Something metallic clicked somewhere close.

I almost ignored it because I was deep in both planning and a sort of melancholy, but old, almost forgotten patterns I'd known well in a long-ago war took over. I rolled over and out of the chair.

Three shots ripped through the screening and spattered whiningly against the brick of the outer walls far above my head.

Inside the house Jo screamed.

I kept rolling away from the source of light inside the house.

I heard running, receding footsteps outside.

"Turn out the lights!" I yelled to Jo.

I went through the screen door low, tearing a hinge away. I had no weapon, but I was very angry. The light went out behind me.

Outside, in the street, all was quiet. A car went past at normal speed and I watched it, but it neither slowed nor speeded so I disregarded it. I listened, waiting for something else.

Nothing came. Then there was something.

A gate banged far down the street. I sprinted that way, moving quickly, toughened to the running by five-mile mornings.

I saw nothing, but two more shots came. The first was high above me, the second closer. I hit the cement and then got up and pounded on, not knowing where I was going. Again there was silence. A block up the street I heard a car start. The engine caught and roared. The driver was in gear and moving away from me while I was still a hundred yards away. I tried to read the license, but couldn't. The car was familiar-looking when it passed the corner streetlight. I knew one like it. I'd spent time night-touring in it back in my unmarried days. I'd played golf and tennis and cards with its owner, been drunk in it, if it was the car I remembered.

Lights had come on all over the neighborhood. I saw people watching me from their doors.

The car vanished around the corner.

I went back home. Jo waited anxiously at our door.

"Are you and the baby all right?"

"Who was it?" she asked, answering my question with her own.

"I got a fair look at the car. I think it might have been Tinker's car."

She shook her head. Her face was gray. "You're crazy. I hope you realize you're crazy. No one else goes chasing after someone shooting at him when the chaser doesn't have even a rock to throw. You tore the screen door down and left me here in the dark. I thought I'd never see you alive again." She reached out a hand and caught mine strongly. "I heard a neighbor yell the police had been called while I was waiting in the dark." She nodded to herself quickly and nervously. I thought she was close to hysteria so I extricated my hand and put my arms around her and held her. She was rigid for a time and then she went limp. "I thought the police would come and I'd have to go out and identify what was left." She shuddered. "Don't do anything like that again. Please?"

"All right," I said soothingly. Now that it was over it was an easy promise.

She continued to hold on to me. "I know you told me not to, but sometimes I forget to unplug the phone after I've called out. There's someone, or maybe several someones, who call, Don. He or they threaten me and the baby."

"Anonymous callers are cowards."

Her grip on me tightened. "They say you better quit digging around and causing problems. It scares me."

"Would you want to move in with your aunt until this trial is over and things have settled down a little?"

"No." She shook her head. "No, I won't let them do that to me."

We stood holding on to each other. In a while a white Bington police cruiser came past outside and parked up the block where I could still see it. An old friend got out, Chief George Gentrup. A uniformed patrolman accompanied him. I watched them from the door. There was enough light outside for George to see me and Jo there.

"Robak?" he called tentatively.

"Come on inside, George."

He came up the walk. I led him to the screened porch. The uniformed officer followed.

"We got a call there was a shooting incident," Gentrup said. "The person who called said you went running after a car like a crazy man after he heard a bunch of shots. I was on station so I came."

I inspected him. His hair was turning white at the edges, but he was still trim. He was a man made of coiled, steel springs and scrap iron, born to be a policeman. He was half mean, sometimes a ranter, and he didn't like lawyers much. I'd known him for a long time, fought and argued with him, and now we normally got along.

"The person I chased drove a car like Tinker Clippage's was three years back," I said.

"Are you telling me one of our good county commissioners tried to shoot you?" he asked.

"I'm saying Tink used to have a car like the one I saw. I don't know whether he still does. Shots were fired at me when I was on my porch. When I went outside I got fired on again. The last thing I saw was a car which I thought was Tinker's buzzing off."

"What kind of gun?"

"Small caliber I'd guess, but I don't know."

"What makes you say 'small caliber'?"

"It didn't make a lot of noise, George."

"Do you intend to try to file charges against Tinker?" he asked curiously.

I thought for a moment. "I know how it works, George. I'm not going to try to do anything tonight. I realize, if I do try to do something, it has to go through Herman. I'll see him in the morning in court. I'd like for you and your officer to cover the neighborhood and look for witnesses. Tink's face has been on the front page of the *Chronicle* even more than yours. A lot of people know him. Someplace someone may have seen him or gotten the license number on his car, if it was him and his." I watched his face, but as usual couldn't read a thing. He'd survived political change in a political town for a dozen years because he was unreadable, good at the job, and nonpartisan.

"I subpoenaed Tink in a case we're trying in court. It upset him when I did. I know that for a fact. I talked with him on the phone and he was upset enough to threaten me."

"I've heard about your trial, Robak. You're hotter in town than a fox in a forest fire." He shook his head. "Knowing what I know about it, my guess is it would be stupid for the commissioner to come here after you with a gun, Robak."

"Fear isn't bright."

"My problem is that I'm never sure where you're coming from. They've got your client tied and ready to deliver. All your trial's for is to see how much his sentence will be. To burn or not to burn. Even if he burns you lawyers will fight over what the voltage should

be. Not that he'll ever fry given the state of things your supreme
court has dictated."

I nodded. "I hope you're right as far as Ed Sager is concerned."

"I'm right. How come you started throwing in all this other stuff
I've been hearing about?"

"I made a deal to plead Sager out and Herman backed up on
me." I looked out into the night. The house lights in the neighborhood were going off. "It's an election year."

He nodded. "We'll check out the neighborhood. Stan can take
the far side of the street and little old me, I'll take this side." His
eyes came back to me. "I'm going to call the prosecutor. I'll tell
him, if he wants, that he can call Tinker. That way everyone knows
where things stand. I'll do my call first off, soon as we finish check-
ing here. I'll report to the prosecutor what we found."

"One thing then, George. I'm going to keep a watch. If I should
see Tinker Clippage in or around this neighborhood, or even see a
yellow county truck come through, I just might figure he came back
to finish the job or sent someone to do it for him. I'll then act
accordingly."

"What's 'act accordingly' mean?" he asked quizzically. He held
up a hand before I could answer. "I heard a guy say something like
that a month or two ago. Maybe you read in the *Chronicle* about
him. He's the one who claimed the neighborhood gangs were bothering him. He got out his shotgun and fired it a night or two after he
complained. He got his own kid and one other. They both lived, but
nothing will ever be the same. You get problems you call us."

"And Herman Leaks?" I asked. "My wife and baby live here in
this house with me, George."

"Look closer," George said reasonably, leading me to the screen.
"Your potshooter wasn't trying to puncture you, at least with his first
shots, or else he's the world's worst shot. See where the slugs came
through? High up. You were sitting five or six feet below." He shook
his head. "He shot to scare you." He smiled very slightly. "I'd guess
that didn't work out. He'd have to be as dumb as you to think it
would work. You've got a Mount Rushmore head, harder than gran-
ite."

I inspected the holes in the screen. George Gentrup was right.

There were three of them and they were almost at ceiling height in the screen, closely spaced together.

Gentrup formally shook my hand. "Sleep well," he said ironically. "Your Bington police force will be on the watch." He opened the damaged porch door and walked out into the night.

I stood there and thought about myself. A few years back, without responsibilities such as I now owned, I might have gone out to prowl the bars of Bington seeking Tinker Clippage. If age hadn't made me wiser it had at least changed my priorities. I took Jo and Joe and went to bed. They slept. I tried to sleep without success. I wondered why Tinker had come. Was he afraid of the questions I'd ask? What did he know about Beth I didn't know?

I thought I might get a call from Prosecutor Herman Leaks during the night, but none came, even though I plugged in the phone for once.

I kept drifting off and dreaming about Tinker Clippage. Before he'd been one of several. Now he'd singled himself out.

I awoke at dawn and got up and ran five miles.

I came back home for a shave and shower, a solitary egg on unbuttered toast, and black coffee. Several times I saw Bington police cruisers pass by in front and that was some comfort.

I walked to the courthouse.

Steinmetz awaited me at our counsel table. He was bright and cheerful and he wore his blue pinstripe suit, the one that was still solid at the elbows. Even Ed Sager, when the unsmiling deputy delivered him, seemed glad to see Steinmetz. He mumbled and nodded at the old judge. Steinmetz's imperious look made the intrusive deputy back up ten feet away from our counsel table to keep his watch.

"I hear you had problems last night. Half the town's telling it. Some of them like the telling. I also hear Chief Gentrup didn't find any decent witnesses, but also Tinker still is driving the same car."

"How'd you hear all that?"

Steinmetz looked over at the door. "Hold on about that for now. Here comes Herman."

Leaks came bustling in followed by his entourage of deputies. He nodded coolly at me and smiled obsequiously at Steinmetz. Despite the smile, we all knew he hated Steinmetz. He still seemed determined to show a constant, good face to him.

"Good morning, sir," he said. He held out a hand and Steinmetz grinned and shook it.

When they disengaged hands Steinmetz held up his and counted. "One, two, three, four, five fingers. Yep, all there. How, Herman. Dug up any old bodies lately?"

Herman's smile weakened. He turned abruptly to me. "I hear you had a minor problem last night."

"Correct. I'd like some further investigation into it."

Herman nodded carefully. "We'll see. The way I hear it you have nothing. You didn't see anything. Nothing. You'd issued all those silly subpoenas and made some citizens edgy, very edgy. Maybe one of them was coming to reason with you, just sort of passing by, and saw you sitting on your porch. What with your notorious temper your caller took his gun. Maybe the gun even went off accidentally."

"Yeah, three times. Two more later."

"It could have been a repeater," he said stoutly, as if that explained it. "But you don't know whose repeater."

"I thought maybe you might, Herman. What you're telling me is there'll be no investigation, no more questions?"

"Definitely."

I smiled and turned my back on him. I winked at Steinmetz. I could see Leaks out of the corner of my eye. He turned away and then nervously turned back again.

"I don't want any fuss made about this," he ordered solemnly.

"Screw you and the writ you rode up on, Herman," I said. "I don't give a damn what you want."

He looked more nervous, but he stood his ground. "There's not a thing you can do about it. My office is constitutional. I make the final decision about what to do and what not to do."

"Go talk with your deputies or read a lawbook," I said. "Maybe you can get some idea of what I plan to do."

"I've already done my research," he said. "So you file some kind of lawsuit? So what?"

"My plan is to make you a defendant, Herman. That way I can

find out what you know about this. I think you know more than Chief Gentrup and more than me."

"You can't do that. I wasn't there."

Steinmetz intervened gently. "Robak knows that, Leaks." He was grinning widely now. "Haven't you ever heard of a conspiracy?" He nodded at me and I saw the tiny wink. "That's what Don and I worked on earlier this morning figuring you'd not do anything to embarrass one of your political pals in what might be a bad election year for you."

"The people Robak subpoenaed are or were friends of yours, too, Judge Steinmetz," Leaks said, his face gone pale.

"They aren't anything to me but public enemies when one of them or someone else aided and abetted by one or more of them goes hunting for my law partners," Steinmetz answered harshly. "Ask your little hired helpers at your counsel table if they ever heard of a 'special prosecutor' in law school, assuming they've been there?"

"I'll talk this over with them and get back to both of you later," Leaks said intently. "You know I want to do what's right, Judge." He shook his head and for a moment I thought he might cry. "Sometimes I'm sorry I ever heard of this case. Diaries, subpoenas, the damned phone ringing, people telling me what to do."

"Sure," Steinmetz said soothingly. "We know it's bad on you and Don and I know you always want to do the right thing. It's just that there are impediments and problems for you in doing it." He nodded. "I hear your primary opponent is still screaming about some votes he claims you bought in May. I also hear there may be a ton of law watching the polls in November."

"Who told you that?"

"I don't remember," Steinmetz said. He leaned a little toward Herman. "Confidentially, I hear you'd better win for the sake of both your body and soul, Herm."

Leaks nodded abstractedly and turned away. When he was out of earshot I said, "What was that all about? I know you were kidding him about our conference, but what's this about his election?"

He answered my question with one of his own. "Would you really want to prosecute Tinker Clippage?"

"I don't know. Maybe I would, maybe not. I can punish him just by calling him as a witness here, letting the newsboys know a bit about it quietly, and then laying all over him on the stand. And it makes me angry that Tinker could rightly figure not much would happen if he was caught." I shook my head. "But I guess he wasn't really trying to shoot me anyway. He shot way over my head when I was on the porch. He could have shot me when I chased him, but didn't. And I remember he used to hunt squirrels with a rifle."

"I heard that also."

"From whom?" I asked, fascinated at how he seemed always to know what was going on in Bington and Mojeff County.

"You know I never reveal sources. That keeps me learning lots. Let's leave the pot at boil and see what happens. Tink's another reason why we can get something up the line just for backing a little away."

"Okay, but what's this about the election?"

"The word's around that Herman personally bought votes in the primary and paid for what he bought by delivering the cash himself. His primary opponent apparently has some affidavits signed by people Herman paid. My guess is if Herm doesn't win in November he might wind up getting indicted."

I could believe it, knowing Mojeff County politics. I nodded.

"Back to the battle," Steinmetz said. "What's up for the day?"

I looked down at the prosecutor's witness list. "My feeling is it'll be time for them to call the various doctors. There are three doctors, two from the local hospital. They examined Beth when she was brought there and pronounced her dead, which she undoubtedly was. There's also a pathologist from out of town whom the coroner and the prosecutor hired at extravagant expense."

Steinmetz gave me a questioning look full of impatience. "The names, Robak. The names."

"Oh, sorry. The two locals are Dr. Lee Ryan and Dr. Ed Swarendon. Do you know them?"

"Sure, sure. I've been sick so many times in my life that every doctor in Bington has felt of my pocketbook. I know Ed and Lee."

"Do you want to do cross on them?"

"Not particularly. I'll leave that in your hopelessly inept hands. You've lived the case. Who's Herman's pathologist?"

"A Dr. Hugo Platz. I've a copy of his report here in the file. They brought him in from the big city, or, more accurately, transported the body to the city for him to do the examination. I didn't depose him for obvious reasons."

"You mean because he's merely an added attraction for Herman to parade before the jury?"

"Yes."

A peculiar look passed over Steinmetz's face. Sometimes he looked like he was eating lemons. "Dr. Platz testified in my court several times. He's good, rather a pompous ass, but good." He nodded to himself, deciding. "If you'd like for me to take someone on cross-examination then I'll take him. Whether I do or not I want to be in the courtroom when he testifies, whether it's today or some other day."

"I want you here for whatever time you can give it," I said. "And sure, you can do cross on him." I was a little puzzled. No one makes many points fooling with pathologists in murder cases. They keep mentioning things you really don't want the jury to hear. I dug through my file and came up with Platz's report. "Here's what I've got. It isn't much."

He gave what I had a swift perusal and handed it back. He looked out the windows of the courthouse. Outside, the squirrels were already at morning games in the trees.

"I'd never have lasted two terms without those squirrels," Steinmetz said.

CHAPTER SEVEN

Rules of Procedure: Trials of persons accused of crime shall continue day by day until the court and jury have heard all proper matters.

The bailiff entered and said, "All rise."

We stood and Judge Harner came in. He nodded coolly out at Leaks and me and gave Steinmetz a smile.

"Good to see you, Judge," he said, looking out into his courtroom where hushed spectators stood waiting patiently for him to begin the proceedings of the day.

"Likewise," Steinmetz said, smiling amiably.

"Sometimes I wish you were up here and I was back out there," Harner said in a low voice, his smile diminishing.

"Stick with it," Steinmetz said. "It tends to get better."

Harner nodded. "Ready for the day to begin, gentlemen?"

"Prosecution is ready," Leaks said.

"Defense is ready," I said.

The judge nodded at the bailiff. "Bring the jury in."

The bailiff opened the jury door and led the jury in. They took their seats and sat waiting.

"Call your next witness, Mr. Prosecutor," Judge Harner ordered.

"The state calls Dr. Hugo Platz," Herman said. He came lightly over to our counsel table and whispered, "He's a little out of order, but he's here, he's costing the county money, so I'm using him first if you've no objections."

Steinmetz smiled. "Let's see, Herm. I remember you used to like to call your best witness of the day in the morning before the other side woke up. I've heard Platz testify before. I'll be doing the cross on him." His answer was in a low voice so the jury wouldn't hear.

"Fine with me," Herman said loudly. He smiled down at us, once again beaming with good spirits on the surface. I wondered again what made him tick. He seemed to me to be almost a completely political creature. He was married to old Bington money, he dressed expensively, and I'd heard he played fair tennis. He and I didn't frequent many of the same cocktail parties and I was happy that way. Maybe he had outside friends? Most lawyers I knew hated him, but perhaps he had his following someplace. I'd just never found that place. *Never-never land.* He'd tried once for state office, but it had ended disastrously. The bar still grinned about that. And now trouble seemed ahead if he wasn't reelected.

Dr. Platz came in and Judge Harner swore him. He took the witness stand. The doctor was relaxed, fortyish, sharp-featured, and wearing casual clothes. He wore checked red-and-blue pants, an open shirt, and loafers. He affected little half-glasses, upper part cut off. His answers, as Herman questioned him, were quick and precise and without wasted words. Beside me I could see Steinmetz watching him intently, taking in every word.

"You did the autopsy on Beth Sager, Doctor Platz?" Leaks asked after qualifying the witness.

"Yes. I had two assistants. Present in the room at the time of the autopsy in addition to my two assistants was your sheriff, one Abraham Dorsett. I gave the bullet fragment, when it was extracted, to Sheriff Dorsett after I'd marked it."

Leaks held up a little plastic vial, already marked by the court. In it a tiny fragment of metal gleamed. I'd seen the exhibit before at an omnibus hearing. It was part of a slug and it had been taken from Beth Sager.

"Where did you discover this fragment in Beth Sager's body?"

I could have objected, but Steinmetz was to have Platz on cross so I gritted my teeth. Steinmetz listened, bemused seemingly.

"May I first describe its path?" Dr. Platz asked politely.

"Of course," Herman said, smiling.

Again I wanted to break up their tête-à-tête, but an imperious glance from Steinmetz cured me. "Let it go, Robak, I've seen this cookie in action before. All you'll do is get frustrated going after him now. And look over the jury?"

I did look. They were hanging on Platz's every word.

"The slug went in at the extreme upper end of her nose," Platz said. "She was shot directly between the eyes. The bone is heavier above than it is at the nose. In fact the nose is cartilage. The bullet drove bone splinters into her brain and a piece of the projectile near the top broke off and lodged above the exit wound. I found it there." He smiled some more. "I suspected it was there. Your police officer had found the rest of the spent slug in a wall, but part of it was gone. I suspected it had remained with her. So I found it." He took the vial with the tiny piece of metal in it, which Leaks handed him. "That's the one. Through the plastic I can see the tiny mark I put on it to identify it."

"What was the cause of Beth Sager's death?"

"The passage of the bullet through her head caused massive shock. Its exit point was just above the brain stem. There was more massive shock. I'd say, as a result, her heart stopped, ceased beating." Dr. Platz shook his head gravely. "If the shock hadn't done it then she'd have died quite soon from the wound itself."

"How soon, in your expert medical opinion, Doctor Platz, did the wound kill her after it was inflicted?"

"I'd say within seconds."

"Within seconds?" Leaks repeated, making it a new question.

I was getting more and more irritated, but Steinmetz shook his head and I let it go.

Leaks offered the exhibit. Steinmetz nodded it in without objection and it was duly and gingerly passed to the jury members. I saw several of them raising the vial to the light to see Dr. Platz's tiny mark at the bottom of the fragment. I'd seen it before. I sighed.

Platz sat calmly back in the witness chair, smiling slightly. The bullet came back to Leaks from the last juror.

"Your witness, gentlemen," Leaks said sleekly.

Steinmetz smiled and got up. "Doctor Platz, it's nice to see you again."

Platz inclined his head.

"I've heard you testify before, haven't I?"

"A number of times," Platz said, satisfied about it.

"I've always found you to be thorough, Doctor. How long, for example, did you spend examining the body of Mrs. Beth Sager?"

"I have my full notes on it here. May I look at them?" Dr. Platz asked politely.

"Surely," Steinmetz said. "Are those the same notes Mr. Robak and I were furnished?"

Platz shook his head, not knowing. He opened his file. "We started examining the body of Mrs. Sager at 10:32 in the morning of March 23 and finished at 11:55 that same day."

"Morning or evening?"

"Morning of course," Platz said, his voice a bit frosty.

"And did you spend all that approximate hour and a half tracing the path of the bullet and looking for the fragment you suspected existed?"

"Of course not."

"What else did you do, Doctor Platz?"

"We examined the body for other wounds. There were none. We did the normal things we do in any autopsy. The deceased was a white, caucasian female in her late thirties, well nourished, in good physical shape." He smiled a little. "That's about all of interest I can tell you."

"Nothing else?"

Platz shrugged. In the background, behind them, I saw Herman Leaks rise.

"The witness has answered, your honor."

Judge Harner nodded. "Let's move on."

Steinmetz said, "May I see your notes, Doctor Platz?"

Leaks was still up. "They're work product, your honor. We provided the defense with a copy of Doctor Platz's medical report."

"And I'd like now to see the notes," Steinmetz rejoined. "The doctor has used them. That makes them available to us."

"Show him the notes, Doctor Platz," Judge Harner ordered.

Platz obediently handed his file to Steinmetz. Steinmetz brought them to our counsel table and put them between us. I tried to read them as Steinmetz read them. He was faster than me. I'd get about halfway down a page and Steinmetz would turn it. He finished, got up, and handed the pages back to Dr. Platz. He looked back at our table and smiled at me and also at Ed Sager, who was watching with empty eyes.

"There are several things in the report you didn't tell the jury, aren't there, Doctor?"

"What's that?" Platz asked. "I left nothing out about the cause of Mrs. Sager's death. That's what I was called here to testify concerning."

"True enough. But did you tell the jury she was about ten weeks pregnant at the time of her death?"

I heard a little hum go through the spectators and I saw Ed Sager's head jerk. For the first time since the trial had begun he started to look as if he was interested.

"That's not a completely unusual condition in a woman her age."

"Did you tell the prosecution about it?"

"I don't recall," Platz said, pursing his lips. "Perhaps. Perhaps not."

"Did you talk with the prosecutor before the trial?"

"One time on the phone."

"Did he tell you anything about the defense plans in this trial?"

"No," Platz said, shaking his head emphatically.

"Beth Sager was ten weeks pregnant?"

"Yes, sir. She was."

Beside me Ed Sager plucked at my sleeve. I turned to him. His eyes, for the first time, weren't empty. They sparked with anger.

"She hated kids," he said, low-voiced. "She said a thousand times she wasn't going to have any little house apes around her. She hated my son until he got big enough for her to make a kind of pass at him." He shook his head, clearing it. "Then, I didn't believe him, I believed her. If she was ten weeks pregnant on March 19 when she died it wasn't my kid. I wasn't in her bed for at least six months and maybe more before then."

"Look over the book I tried to show you earlier," I said. "It should be more interesting to you now." I remembered something. The last date in the book had been in November. "Try to remember if she was going with any of the men in the book when she might have gotten pregnant."

"I don't know," he said. "It's all so foggy." He reached out. "Let me see the book."

I handed him a copy and he began to thumb through it.

I saw the jury had noticed his unusual animation and now were curious about the book, watching it, and not watching Dr. Platz. Steinmetz, aware of what was happening, had moved to a place at the side of the jury and was standing there quietly.

"Are you done, Mr. Steinmetz?" Judge Harner asked. His face was polite, a mask made for the courtroom, showing nothing.

"Perhaps so, your honor," Steinmetz said. He looked at Sager and then at me, his brows raised in question. I shrugged, not knowing.

"Could we break for a few moments before I decide?" Steinmetz asked.

"Of course, Mr. Steinmetz," Harner said. He cautioned the jury and sent them to the jury room. Several of them were still staring curiously at Ed Sager as they passed our counsel table.

We conferred.

"You're telling us you had no relations with your wife for at least six months before she was killed?" I asked, when the jury door closed.

Ed Sager shook his head. "Longer than that probably. She booted me out. She'd done it lots before. She'd go to her lawyers and get an order giving her the house and for me to pay her money. Even if I didn't pay it, and sometimes I didn't, that didn't make any difference to her. She had her own money, family money. She'd use her money and then charge it back to me. The times she took me back one of the conditions was I had to pay her back. I paid her. I was always glad to pay her." He looked down at the table. "I was drinking and I'd been drinking for days or weeks maybe. The business had gone to hell because I'd quit watching it or caring about it. I went out to the house in the afternoon. I almost drove my car off the road, but I made it out there."

"On the day she was killed?" I asked.

He nodded. "We argued some. I remember that. She said she was going to go ahead with the divorce this time. She told me to leave and I left for a while. I left the car and walked some down by the river. I had me some more to drink from a flask I carry. I thought maybe then I could go back to the house and talk to her some more, make some sense out of it. So I went back." He shook his head again. "Things are confused from then on. Next thing I can, for sure, remember is coming out of it when I saw her body. I saw the gun there. I drank some more, I guess. I don't remember the sheriff, but I do remember sounds, the clicking, sounds . . ." He looked at us, seeking belief. "She wasn't pregnant with my child. Maybe I still shot her." He looked imploringly at Steinmetz. "Maybe she told me and I got mad and shot her and just can't remember it or why I did it."

"You remember what you're telling us now, don't you?" Steinmetz asked.

"I remember a little." Ed shook his head like a man coming up from deep, cold water. "Are you saying if I remember that part I'd remember shooting her?"

Steinmetz nodded. "I guess, but I'm not an expert in the field." He looked over at me. "What's in the diary for the critical times, Don?"

"Nothing on any of our available witnesses, but it does look like a good question to ask them all. You know. Point a finger and ask all of them if they're papa. The diary cuts off before the first of December. That's George Pitchford time."

"No late December or early January dates listed?"

"Nope."

"Maybe she gave me a Christmas gift and I forgot," Ed said plaintively. He shook his head. "There's holes in my brain. The docs said there would be if I didn't quit. Could I have forgot that?"

"We can't worry about what you might have done," Steinmetz answered him gently. He tapped Ed on the hand. "What Robak and I want you to do, from this time forward, is sit here beside us, listen hard, and tell us if anything occurs that reminds you of something or sounds wrong. Will you do that, Ed?"

"Sure," he said. "I know it's too late now." He turned to me. "I guess I was just being funny about Christmas, Don. I know it's too late for me now, but it wasn't my kid she was carrying. I want to tell the jury that."

I could see spectators leaning to hear what we said and I knew

Herman Leaks so well that I was suspicious of everything and everyone. "Lower your voice, Ed. Herman could have someone in the spectator area."

Steinmetz nodded in agreement. "Why'd you keep admitting over and over you'd done it?"

"Who else could it have been?" Sager asked simply. "I guess it was me. I was drunk and confused that day."

"The sheriff said you seemed as usual," Steinmetz said.

"The only time the sheriff ever saw me was when I was drunk."

I nodded. "The diary and her pregnancy give us some other answers about who might have done it. They aren't good answers, but they're worth pursuing."

Ed nodded back. "Everything is blurry for me. Sometimes something will be there for me and I'll want to remember it, but I seldom can reach it."

"Keep trying. And listen to the testimony."

Judge Harner tapped his gavel lightly against the bench. "You gentlemen about ready?"

I looked at Steinmetz and he nodded he was ready. Dr. Platz retook the witness stand and the jury was brought back in.

"A few more questions, Doctor," Steinmetz said smoothly. "Did you do a blood alcohol test on Beth Sager?"

"Yes."

"What were the results of that test?"

Herman Leaks got up. "Your honor, of what possible use could evidence of that nature be?"

"Are you objecting, Mr. Leaks?"

"I'm objecting."

"Overruled."

Steinmetz asked again, "What were the results of that test?"

"She tested point one seven."

"In this state, Doctor Platz, are you aware of the level where the law presumes a person to be under the influence of alcohol?"

"I am, Mr. Steinmetz."

"What is that level?"

"Point one."

"And Beth Sager was considerably beyond that level?"

"Yes."

"Legally drunk?"

Dr. Platz glanced over at Herman Leaks. When no objection came he said, "Yes, sir."

Steinmetz pondered that by thumbing through some notes he was holding. He let the jury ponder it with him during the pause.

"One more question, Doctor Platz," Steinmetz said. "Did you do any tests on Beth Sager to determine whether or not she'd had sexual relations in the hours before she died?"

"No, sir." Platz gave Steinmetz a nasty look. "We weren't asked to do anything like that."

"Yet you found she was pregnant?"

"The tests aren't similar."

"All right then, Doctor. Thank you." Steinmetz turned away. He gave me the tiniest wink and turned quickly back. "One additional thing. When the victim is a woman and murder is suspected or apparent, about how many times, say out of a hundred, are you asked to do tests to determine if there have been sexual relations near the time of death?"

"I can't tell you a percentage, but many times we're asked to do it," Dr. Platz said.

"Thank you, Doctor," Steinmetz said. "That's all."

Herman Leaks got up from his table and approached Dr. Platz.

"Let's take some time and go back over what you *did* find concerning the death of Beth Sager . . ."

"Objection," Steinmetz said. "Learned counsel for the state well knows that redirect is not for the purpose of going back over previous testimony about which there's been no cross-examination, but which he believes is favorable to his case."

"Objection sustained," the judge said.

Leaks turned his back on the bench and spread his hands to the jury as if to tell them and the spectators behind them he was being unfairly treated.

"Mr. Leaks," the judge said. "I hope it's not too much of a burden to you to remain within what are known as the rules of evidence. I witnessed your little gesture just now and I'm going to advise you not to make it or anything like it again in this courtroom.

I'm also now going to admonish the jury to disregard it." He looked out at the jury. "Mr. Leaks was attempting to reprove facts already in evidence through the same questions he'd asked before of the same witness. The court isn't being unfair in not allowing that. This court can't and won't permit either the state or the defendant to do that. Otherwise you, as jurors, might sit here for weeks listening to the same thing from the same witness over and over."

Leaks sat down. He mumbled something to a deputy.

"Nothing else," he said finally.

The first of the two local doctors was called next. His testimony was low-key and routine. He'd examined Beth Sager when an emergency ambulance had delivered her to the hospital at four o'clock. Basically his testimony was that she was dead and had been that way for about an hour and a half.

I smiled at him and, with Steinmetz's approval, asked nothing.

Noon arrived.

CHAPTER EIGHT

Steinmetz's law: *"It's remotely possible that some people might not tell the truth on the witness stand."*

I'd made arrangements the Friday before with Doc Bill Tyne to meet him at the downtown Moose for lunch so Steinmetz and I walked there. As we arrived Tyne was approaching from the other way so we waited for him at the door. I supposed he'd walked. He was as big at walking as I was at running. It kept him fit. He looked very good.

"You don't look sleepy today," I said kiddingly when he got close to us.

He smiled, understanding the remark. "Ask Judge Steinmetz whether one should call at such an hour on Saturday."

Steinmetz grinned and shrugged.

We went inside and found a table.

When we were seated Tyne looked us both over carefully. "You gentlemen make me think you've at least learned where the canary is caged."

"It became a brand-new trial this morning," I said. "We now have us a client who wants to get off and suddenly isn't sure whether or not he did the deed."

Tyne's eyes widened in wonderment. "How the hell did you manage that? He was so despondent and disoriented last time I saw him I wasn't sure he'd ever surface again. I prescribed some mood elevators, but I don't know whether he ever got them or is taking them." He shook his head. "Maybe he'd go for being hypnotized now? Tell me what you want asked and under what conditions you want it asked and I probably could set it up under tight control at the hospital."

"We'll think about it," I said.

"In the meantime I could use either or both of you in the wards up there." He leaned toward us. "Tell me what happened?"

"He found out today that his wife was pregnant when she died and he says the child couldn't have been his," Steinmetz said.

The waitress came. We looked over the brief menus and gave our orders. Our waitress was young, long-haired, and neat-looking. She was interested in Tyne. She batted long-lashed eyes at him, touched his hand once, managed to push a breast into his shoulder, and had a difficult time getting all our orders right.

"Why is it," Steinmetz asked, "that young girls like that smile at you lads and break into open laughter at the sight of me?"

"She wasn't after me," I said. "But if I were Bill here I'd protect myself."

Doc Tyne smiled calmly, unaffected.

"Look, Bill," I said. "We think Ed's story is due for a significant change. I'd thought about not putting him on the stand, but now I will. Once on the stand we believe he'll say he was there, drunk, remembers nothing, and doesn't believe he did it. He'll admit all the stories he told the police and say he was so desperately despondent at finding Beth dead he just gave the police whatever they wanted. Is any of this a problem for you?"

"I suppose not," Tyne said, unsure about it.

Steinmetz drew his chair closer. "He'll also talk about his several tries at suicide. Don and I think we can get mileage out of those." He gave Tyne an inquiring look. "You knew her. How about the chance she might have committed suicide before Ed wandered again into the scene and found her?"

"How about the closet?"

"The closet?" I asked, not remembering for a moment.

"The way I heard it is they found a place where Ed had hidden sometime."

"But there's no time established on it except by Ed's statements, which he'll repudiate."

Tyne shrugged, his eyes unsure. "Suicide is a possibility, but improbable in this case, Judge Steinmetz. Beautiful women take pills, they overdose with drugs, but they seldom blow holes in their lovely heads. I'd say your chances of getting a jury to believe in Beth's suicide are quite remote. However, under the circumstances, it's worth a try."

"Then if you were asked, during your testimony, if she could have committed suicide, what would you answer?"

Dr. Tyne thought about it. "I suppose I'd say it was possible. She ran highs and lows. She wasn't a manic-depressive, but she was close, borderline if you will."

"Did she tell you she was pregnant?" I asked curiously.

"No." He shook his head. "There were times when I sensed there were facts she wasn't telling me, things she was keeping inside herself for reasons of her own. She was upset and she was uptight the last time I saw her. I think it had slowed her down some."

"But you didn't know why?" I asked.

He shook his head.

"If she didn't want the baby are there places around where she could easily have had it aborted?"

"There are a number of them. A bright, sophisticated woman like Beth Sager would have had no problem."

"For some reason she didn't do that," I said, thinking about it. "Figure that out for me."

He shook his head.

Steinmetz said, "If she did nothing about it then we'll have to guess she wanted, for some as yet unknown reason, to keep the baby."

The whole thing perplexed and puzzled me. Beth had hated kids, at least according to Ed Sager. She'd wanted none and had none. Then suddenly, estranged from her husband, having been recently involved in numerous affairs, and nearing the end of her childbearing years, she'd allowed herself to get pregnant, then done nothing about it. *Love?*

I pulled a copy of the diary out of my pocket. "There's not much here. Most of her affairs seemed to have been over last fall. There was one stranger we can't figure out. His name was George Pitchford. I asked you about him on the phone, Doc."

"She mentioned his name, but that's all I know about him. The best information I can give you is that a couple of days before her

death she told me she was going through with the divorce. I asked
her if that meant a new man and she smiled and said she hoped it
did. She'd said that sort of thing before and it hadn't meant anything, so I didn't pay a great deal of attention to it." He thought for
a moment. "If your book shows a George Pitchford and he's the
new man then maybe he'd be important. I just don't know."

Steinmetz nodded. "We'll have someone in the office go to the
telephone company and check white pages for the cities around
here," I said. "And maybe we could also check some out-of-state city
directories. The dates in her book would indicate that all their meetings weren't on weekends. So he might be calling on the trade
here." I looked at Tyne again. "When she took off on weekends
where all would she go?"

"She'd drive as far as Chicago at times. Cincinnati, Indianapolis,
Louisville, St. Louis. Or she might go to one of the nearby cities and
fly out for a few days. She had wads of money of her own, maybe
some of it from what she squirreled away when Ed was going good.
She could put on enough diamonds to blind you."

I sighed and nodded. "What she probably did, but I don't want
to admit it, is take up with someone else and not put it in her diary.
Or maybe things got serious enough with George Pitchford or someone else before or after him that she just stopped her entries. On the
sticks where she kept score there's no way of knowing when those
times were after the last date in the diary."

Steinmetz nodded. "Maybe it stopped being a game for her."

"Does that stop us from pointing the finger at each of our reluc-
tant witnesses and saying 'Daddy' to them?"

"Hell no," Steinmetz said. He smiled at both of us. "We'll point
the vindictive, accusing finger at each and every one of them. We'll
ask them if they were with her in December or January. We'll ask
them, if they say no, if they know who was. We'll ask them who they
saw her with, what she said, what she did. It should maybe lead to
some interesting answers."

Tyne nodded. He looked away and then back. "Does this mean
you're abandoning your insanity defense?"

I shook my head. "Not at all. The most we ever had in this case
was a bucket of zilch." When I saw his puzzlement I went on.

"Think about it, Doc. Let's say Ed Sager became self-protective
after the fact of murder. Let's say he'd then shut up, made no
statements, and called loudly for a lawyer. Would it have made any
difference? I believe a grand jury would still have indicted him because Herman Leaks had the goods on him. He was sitting in the
same room with his dead wife with the gun that killed her in his
hand, there'd been some kind of fight or struggle, there was some
evidence he'd hidden even if the time couldn't be established, and
he was where he'd been ordered not to be. So his statements hurt,
but not that much. They had him anyway. We began way behind.
Yours was our only defense when Ed was the way he was."

Tyne frowned. "But now things have changed?"

Steinmetz nodded, taking my place in the discussion. "What we
want to do now, in the defense, is to show Ed maybe didn't kill her,
but that she committed suicide. Or we show if Ed did kill her that
he had good reason. Or we show that if he killed her he was insane
or so intoxicated that he couldn't form the intent for the deed. We
don't care which one the jury buys. Probably they'll buy none of
them, but put all together we don't think a jury will rap Ed hard."

"We hope," I added.

"But I'm still going to testify the way we talked about before."

"Mostly. Your answers shouldn't change much because of new
facts or because now Ed's decided he maybe didn't kill his wife.
That fits in as well with your theories, or almost as well, as what you
had before, doesn't it?"

"I suppose," Tyne said, frowning.

"Is his change of attitude that puzzling to you?" Steinmetz asked.

"I guess not," Tyne said. "Ed's a man with a son, a man who
wanted more children, if I can believe what he said to me. He lived
for years with Beth. She told him she'd have no children and wanted
none. Suddenly he finds she's let herself become pregnant and that
he's not the father. She's done something with another person she
wouldn't do with him even in the early days of their marriage. It
changed his thinking on her, it diminished her, and it may have
made him finally hate her. During their life together he wanted to
dominate her, but was unable to make that work. Instead she decided things, she controlled. The only way he could escape that and

the other things he saw happen in their marriage was to drink, so he drank and then drank more." He shook his head. "That made things worse. That let her live as she pleased. Still, Ed loved her. I think maybe he still does, but now he also hates her. He took her back countless times despite the men. She didn't even have to promise him better performance." He looked up and smiled. "But today he finds out she's pregnant . . ."

The waitress came bringing soup and sandwiches. Predictably, she served Tyne first. I thought she was panting a bit. Tyne was wearing a soft summer suit. She got behind him and served over his shoulder, getting a breast into it again.

I wondered if Tyne even saw her.

She served me next well enough, then dropped Steinmetz's food in front of him and fled.

Steinmetz grinned.

"So far there hasn't been much from the prosecution that makes me want to dig deep into you, Doc," I said to Tyne. "Hopefully we'll stick pretty much to the stuff you got asked on your deposition."

"Why not just introduce the deposition and publish it?" Tyne asked. "I mean I'm busy."

"No. Real, live doctors are more interesting to jurors than the dry reading of a deposition. Besides, there are women on the jury."

"Am I supposed to show some leg?"

"If you want." I turned to Steinmetz. "Have there ever been any Pitchfords around here, Judge?"

"There used to be a Pitchford family out on Pleasant Ridge when I was a boy. That was fifty or sixty years ago. They've all died out or moved on. The one we're looking for might be a part of the family, but he'd be one from the bunch who moved on."

That looked like a blind alley, so I turned back to Tyne. "Did you start Beth on the crosswords and other things like that, Doc?"

He gave me a quick look. "I thought it was good for her. She had a quick mind, she liked to read, and it kept her off the streets part of the time. Why do you ask?"

"I found some puzzle books in the alcove where I found her diary. In fact, there were books like that all over."

Steinmetz leaned forward. "With luck we'll get someone else to accuse of her murder in the next few days." He nodded at me. "Your pal Tinker Clippage is my number one."

Off and on I'd been thinking about Tink myself. I wondered if he could kill someone who got in his way. Someone like a pregnant Beth, maybe demanding love, honor, and marriage?

That afternoon we got the other local doctor, Lee Ryan. He'd also been on call at the hospital when Beth's body had been delivered. We got descriptions of the wound from him and more pictures of the body. He estimated Beth's time of death at about 2:30, half an hour before the call had come to the sheriff's office. We'd gone over the photos before and so I let the jury see the new ones without objection. Judge Harner was going to let them in anyway and it seemed pointless to object when a long line of solid cases said they were admissible. I'd seen worse get admitted and thereafter be routinely affirmed on appeal.

Leaks seemed to want to use time with Dr. Ryan. I let him lead the doctor through his gory testimony while the jury listened intently. Now and then I'd steal a look at the jury, calculating them. If I was any good at predicting such things my bet was that ex-county councilman McNear would wind up being jury foreman.

Outside it grew hotter. The air-conditioning, as it always did in the old courtroom, began to fail.

The jury sweated. They grew restive.

Leaks led Dr. Ryan on and on.

"And in your medical opinion Beth Sager was long dead when her body was brought to the hospital?" he asked again.

"Yes. That was at 4:30 P.M. and she'd been dead about two hours."

Herman finally quit.

I drew a grateful glance from McNear, who was fanning himself with his hand while I fanned myself with my file, when I said, "No questions," to Dr. Ryan.

Herman then called two emergency medical technicians. They described where and when they'd picked up Beth's body and where they'd delivered it. They were on and off the stand in about ten minutes each.

We asked them no questions.

When the second medical technician was finished Herman asked the court, "May counsel approach the bench?"

"Come up," Harner said, leaning forward.

"I'm out of witnesses for the day," Leaks admitted. "I expected more vigorous cross-examination on the part of the defendant than happened and so I scheduled no one else for the day."

"What'd you expect us to do, Herman?" Steinmetz inquired. "Did you want us to ask your doctor what color her panties were? Did you think we'd fight with him about it being her blood? Did you need us to ask the questions you forgot?"

"I expected you to do a *pro forma* job for your client," Herman said, somehow scandalized.

"Ask your questions again?" Steinmetz inquired icily.

Herman shook his head and I could see he was angry, but then he was always angry when things didn't go the way he'd planned.

"I'm not saying you gentlemen are doing it wrong," he said in a low voice. "I didn't mean it that way."

"Yes you did," Steinmetz said, low-voiced but intense. "You're implying because we didn't ask questions to advance your cause that it's now the defendant's fault you ran out of witnesses. I'm saying that if you're out of witnesses we should be able to assume the state is resting its case."

"No, sir. We're certainly not resting. We have some additional witnesses called for tomorrow. We've got the ballistics man and we have a number of witnesses who saw things happen between the Sagers, lots of things."

Judge Harner nodded patiently. "We'll adjourn until tomorrow morning then. In the morning, Mr. Leaks, you'll have all the rest of your witnesses here and available. If you run dry again I'll find you are resting the state's case." He looked over the edge of the bench at the court reporter. "Put that on the record, Sissy."

Leaks reddened a little, but said nothing.

Steinmetz tapped me approvingly on the arm as we went back to our counsel table.

"How about our witnesses? Any problems? I think Herman will run out tomorrow."

"There could be lots of problems. I subpoenaed people to appear tomorrow, all of them. You can bet some of them won't show, like maybe Tinker Clippage." We both knew that the difference for us, if they didn't appear, would be that we could ask the sheriff to round them up. And, unless Herman was willing to admit what we thought they might say, we could get a continuance until they did appear.

And so our court day ended.

It's said there are no true surprises left these days in a criminal trial, at least in the presentation of the case in chief. Leaks and his people had provided me with the names of all witnesses he expected to call. On those of any importance I'd either deposed them, seen statements from them, or at least interviewed them. So we could now look at the list he'd furnished and see who was left and know basically what they'd testify concerning.

I walked back to the office with Steinmetz. There we retired to my office, which was less cluttered than his.

"He's got the ballistics expert from the state police and six other witnesses to go," I explained to Steinmetz.

"The others are witnesses to scenes in the lives of Beth and Ed?"

"Yep. They'd be people who know about problems in the Sager marriage. Hell, Judge, the world knew that. They'll talk about fights, threats, and the like."

"And that's all he's got left?"

I nodded. "One of them he'll call about Beth and Ed is a lady named Ann Jellicoe. Do you know her?"

He smiled. "I know her. I hear she threw a drink on you at the country club."

"Not exactly. She missed me and got her husband, Chuck." I smiled at him. "Your information is bad." I looked through the file. "I interviewed her a little that night, but there's a written statement in the file. I'd like you to take her. I doubt I can get anything out of her except a sack of venom."

"Happily," he said. He yawned. "Partner Jake called me at home last night and wanted to know how much longer this trial will run. He doesn't like us wasting so much time on criminal matters."

Jake was very efficient and a good partner. He ran the office, something which Steinmetz and I happily let him do. I loved Jake dearly, but had no intention of letting him control my life or my choice of clients.

"Screw Jake," I said.

"And the writ he rode up on," Steinmetz finished for me, grinning. He looked at his watch. "The first shift is about to gather at the Moose. I intend to hie me there. Would you care to join me?"

I shook my head. "I intend to go home tonight without a trace of alcohol on my breath."

"It takes all kinds," Steinmetz said. He got up and waved goodbye from my door.

"Till morning," he said.

I went back to the file. Outside my office window the weather was hot and fine. Our air conditioner ran efficiently. I sat at my desk and thought about the day and the case.

It remained hard for me to believe that a man could kill his wife and fail to remember it, but maybe Ed had or maybe Ed was not being truthful.

Even if someone else, some lover or hater, had done it and I could, at this late date, find it out, it meant nothing. A single, errant thought came about that and I dismissed it before it blossomed into a cloud.

Under current trial procedure the state tomorrow would finish proving its case. I'd be limited, in my defense, in what I could do. I could muddle what they'd done, I could unprove some things they'd proved, and I could try to stir the whole mess into an inedible soup by using the witnesses the state desperately didn't want me to use. The state knew what I had and dreaded it. It wouldn't disprove what Ed had obviously done, but it would give the jurors something to mull on.

I knew what the state had. With the exception of what Steinmetz had unexpectedly dredged out of Dr. Platz, there'd been no surprises. Conversely, the state knew what I had. We'd exchanged witness lists, documents, statements, reports, and pictures, all under the rules regulating discovery.

Trial by ambush was dead and long buried. Of course I had given them a very long list of witnesses and Herman's attention had been primarily directed to the names of his political cronies.

I wondered what those friends would do and say on the stand. Admit all or part? Deny all that was of damage? I thought some of them would do the latter.

A moment of intuition came. I had one thing Herman badly wanted and perhaps I could eat a bit of my cake and save a bit of my cake. Herman wanted some of my witnesses off the testimonial hook. He wanted Beth's diary to become a minor matter. He wanted names to go unmentioned. If it worked for me I could do that—partly.

I wondered idly what he'd trade? *Almost anything?*

The phone rang. I let it ring five times because Jo and I have a code where she calls the office after hours and lets the phone ring three times. Then I call her back. At times, in the office, I don't want to talk with anyone when I'm working late, but men who want to stay married talk to their wives.

Tonight wasn't one of the nights I wanted to avoid the world around me. I answered the phone.

"Robak," a voice I recognized said, "you've got to quit this stinking around in the Sager thing and you've got to get off my back."

"Tell me why I must do that, Mayor?" I asked, intrigued. "I mean you wouldn't even talk to me last Saturday and you told me and a dozen other witnesses you knew nothing about Beth Sager."

"Well, what would you have said?"

"I asked you about making the conversation private."

"I'm sorry about that. Sometimes I think I'm king of the hill at that Saturday breakfast table. But you must know that you and I and the others were victims of that woman just as she was a victim of her husband. She was voracious. She used men and discarded them."

"That's what I have to show to a jury," I said. "Your friend Herman Leaks has my client charged with capital murder because the evidence shows that Ed, or someone, hid in a closet in the house. That's lying in wait. I have to explore every little hole I can come up with in knocking that down."

"That doesn't wash with me, Robak. I talked with Herman. He said he'd offered your client twenty years if he pleaded guilty."

"Not exactly true, Mayor. He sort of offered it, but he didn't get to it in time. After my client accepted the original offer Herman withdrew it. He then offered it again when he saw the new names, yours included, in Beth Sager's little diary." I paused for a moment. "I've got nothing personally against you, but I've got a job and I'm going to do that job."

"Then I have to appear in court tomorrow?"

"If you aren't there the sheriff will go looking for you and the trial will stop until he finds you, Mayor."

He sighed gustily on the phone. "I should have talked to you the other day. My wife's going to come down on me like an Arab on an Israeli."

"Tell me what you know," I said. "Maybe we can do something. I don't want to break up your marriage. I know you once went with Beth. When did it start and stop?"

"Last summer. A year ago. It didn't last long."

"Did you visit her house?"

"Sure." He laughed a little without much humor. "I 'pooled' around some there, if you'll forgive the pun."

"Did you ever hear of a George Pitchford?"

"No. I really didn't. All I knew about with Beth was Beth. I knew other men had been after her and I knew I wasn't her last. I'd sneak past her place after work or after a night meeting. We'd have a few drinks. She'd play games with me like she played them with her puzzles. Was she into things like that when you knew her, Robak?"

"A little," I said, remembering.

"How'd you like for me to call your wife and tell her about you and Beth?" he asked.

"My wife knows. She also knows it happened before we were married," I answered stiffly. "You can do what you want, Mayor. It won't get you off the hook. Something else might. Did you ever see anyone out there when you came, any other man?"

"No. I never saw a car when I'd drive in." He was silent for a moment. "Now and then, when I'd come in the late summer, she'd just put me off and send me on my way. Then, finally, she just quit coming to the door. I'd see her peep out, but she wouldn't open the door for me. So I quit going out there. It hurt my pride a little, but that's been hurt before."

I thought about possibilities. "Wait it out then, Mayor. Don't rattle anything. Don't make any self-serving statements and don't talk to anyone else except Herman. Something just might come along and save you. Before I call you and even Tink I'll talk with Herman some more. That's after he finishes his case, which should be tomorrow."

He was silent for a moment. "When I hit that courthouse hall tomorrow with Tink there'll be reporters coveying around us like maiden ladies around the new male librarian. It'll be sink or swim."

"What if you waited in your office until you were called?"

"That would help a lot. Could I do that?" His voice had grown ingratiating.

"If you promise to be there or be reachable when and if I call?"

"And Tink too?" he asked, asking a question to answer mine. "I heard around that he might have been the one who took some shots at you or might have sent someone to do it. But I got to ask, Don. Me and Tink's buddies. When he come down off the ridges he didn't even wear shoes. Something threatens him or his and he gets downright primitive. And if he'd wanted to puncture you he could have done it."

I thought about it. It seemed a good way to slow things down no matter what I decided later. "Tink, too, but in your office. I'm not sending a client down the tube if you guys can save him."

"How about the others?" he asked.

"Not them," I said. "You tell Herman I'm saving you and Tink to trade with."

"He'll trade," the mayor said. "I know where all his bodies are buried. He better had trade."

I waited for another moment, but he was silent. I rehung the phone.

CHAPTER NINE

Steinmetz's Law: "A defense attorney ain't worth much salt unless he peppers the enemy camp."

I went home. Jo sat in her favorite chair. She was watching her favorite television show. People made love to other people on a cruise liner. Some of them were married. Some of them were even married to each other.

"Dinner's in the oven," she said. "Downtown Moose?"

"Not tonight," I said. "I was at the office late thinking about stuff and looking things over. A witness called and threatened to report to you that I once knew Beth Sager."

"That's old news," she said. "I made an adjustment for that when I married you. If it was afterward that would be something new."

"It wasn't afterward. The witness just thought maybe he could buy himself some restraint with it."

"What's the fascination of digging in old dirt?" she asked, interested for the umpteenth time in my profession. "What makes you and a nice, honest, old man like Steinmetz go into court and fight the world for a rotter like Ed Sager? He's been a perpetual drunk for half a dozen years. In a sane society he'd have been exposed on a rock by now, but not in good, old Bington."

I thought that over as I got meat loaf, potatoes, and carrots out of the oven. They were still warm. Jo watched me carefully, verified for herself I'd not been drinking, and came to help.

"I was sure you'd gone to the Moose with Judge Steinmetz."

I shook my head and got back to the case. "Doesn't a drunk like Ed have as much right to a defense as a sober man?" I asked

"I suppose. I asked you that because I was angry. I expected you home for dinner and you didn't come."

"This trial will be done soon and I'll get back on a regular schedule."

"You look like you've lost ten pounds. Why do trials take so much out of you?"

"You sit and listen to every word. There's a constant state of tension. I'm more worn out from a day of trial than I am from twenty miles of running."

"I see. Well, remember there'll be other trials. There'll always be others, more people like Ed Sager who kill their wives. Just because you can't understand why he did it doesn't make him not guilty."

"His guilt remains, until a jury comes in, unestablished."

"You never give up, do you?" she asked, her voice lightening.

"I prefer to say that I have certain stubborn beliefs." I sat down and began to eat meat loaf and the rest, washing it down with cold water. I was surprised to find I was hungry. Outside, a sudden summer storm blew up with thunder and rain and bolts of bright lightning. I thought of Giles Sager and Ed Jr.

Jo refused to let it go. "You love it, don't you? You love it more than you love me or your son?"

I shook my head. "In trials what I'm doing sometimes consumes me and seems the most important thing there'll ever be, but I recover quickly when the trial is done. I don't love what I do. Sometimes I even hate it. I am *employed* by it. It's what I do, my profession."

She nodded and let up a little. She removed my empty plate and said, "There's Jell-O."

I shook my head. "How did someone hear or see what was going on at the Sager house? It's off the road and it was cold that day, Jo. Yet someone called the sheriff's office about it."

"How do most things get discovered?" she asked in return. "Chance? Accident?"

I ignored her answer/questions. "Ed wandered in early and he was drinking. Beth also had been drinking, at least sometime before she was killed. They didn't drink together. Who did Beth drink with? Did Ed hide sometime that day in the closet? He only remembers drinking by the river and returning. Maybe someone saw him stumbling around down there and used the opportunity. That person might even have guessed or hoped what his reaction would be when he found Beth dead. Maybe someone intended to use him and got very lucky."

She shook her head. "You insist on doing this too much and too often."

"No. Most things are as they seem. Ninety-nine percent of what I do is that way. But this one makes me wonder about other ways it could have happened. If you shot me would you remember it?"

"If I thought I'd be benefited by forgetfulness I might say I didn't remember," she said, smiling at the game I'd named her a player in. "If I'd caught you with Beth Sager after we were married I'd remember, but I'd say I forgot."

"I don't think there's any doubt Ed was in a deep depression," I said. "Why did that make him answer every question he got asked by a uniform?"

"I don't know. What does your psychiatrist think about it?"

"He says Ed was crazy at the time of Beth's death. The other psychiatrists don't completely agree with him, but they do say Ed has some brain damage from heavy drinking." I nodded, more to myself than Jo. "Then there were all these men she was playing crossword games with. Someone got her pregnant and she obviously wanted to get pregnant . . ."

". . . Beth was pregnant when she was killed?"

I nodded.

"How terrible."

"Maybe one of her gentlemen friends, under pressure from her to do something, God knows what, did her in. Then Ed found her and decided in his alcoholic smog that he did her in."

"Isn't it too late for that now?" she asked. "Ed's being tried for it."

"That's true," I admitted. "And the state basically knows most of what I know and I now know about all of what the state knows. It's a dance and each of us is familiar with the proper steps." I looked up at the dining-area wall. It was familiar to me, as well known as the inside of the courtroom. On our wall there were flower pictures and photos of Jo and Joe, me in back of them with an unfamiliar smile. "How can I change the rules?"

"You know you can't and stay a lawyer."

Some possible chancy ways came and I shook my head. "No, that's the wrong answer, Jo. I can't misuse the rules without ethics committee problems, but one's allowed to use them constructively." I smiled at her, feeling a little better, not good, but better. "Maybe there's a way." I thought again for a long moment. "I should show you my witness list. It's two pages, double-spaced. I've no intention of using all or many of those witnesses, but I will use some of them. The trick, in dealing with Herman these days, is in disguising whom you will use. There was no way for the prosecutor to check out all my witnesses in the time he had from when I furnished the list and trial date. Herman's got one overworked investigator and the world of Bington knows Herman isn't going to stoop to that kind of work himself. So I gave him a creative list. I put three people on it I might use for every one I will use."

"That's—that's mean and unfair," she said, scandalized by it.

"When your client can get the death penalty I felt a bit of meanness and unfairness was in order."

She watched me for a moment and then a tiny, small smile came. She came to me and put her hand on mine. "It's like a battle, isn't it? I guess with it being that way I ought to be more on your side and I shouldn't pick so much at you. Sometimes I don't really understand, don't see it through your eyes." Her hand tightened. "I want Joe to get bigger so I can go back to work. Things are more simple there." She squeezed my hand again. "I'll try harder."

"You do just fine," I said.

I took the phone jack out and then slept pretty well, all things considered. I came awake twice after odd dreams where Beth chased me down a dark hall toward a swimming pool I knew was empty. I used those waking periods to plot against tomorrow's light.

In the morning the corridor outside the courtroom was full of people. Ann Jellicoe sneered at me as I passed her, but I ignored her. She stood dumpily but regally in the hall and I heard her tell some acquaintance she'd rather be playing golf.

Spectators, hoping perhaps the fireworks would begin today in earnest, were more numerous than ever when court convened.

If they expected big things early I'm sure they were disappointed with the state's first witness of the day. He was Captain Robert Lemon Sandy of the state police, the department's semiretired, on-call ballistics expert. He'd brought his slides and projector, and the judge, at Herman's request, ordered the courtroom darkened after the equipment was set up. I decided not to ask for the popcorn concession.

Captain Sandy, his old, puckered face emotionless, described how he'd gotten possession of the slug that had killed Beth Sager, how and where he'd gotten the gun, and the tests he'd done, and what also he'd done thereafter to preserve the custody chain.

Sandy was a thin, small man, very precise in his speech, now sixty-plus years old. I'd had him in court before and knew the best way to treat him. Despite the fact that a sliver had come off the slug and lodged in Beth's brain, I wasn't about to argue that Beth hadn't been killed by a shot fired from the .38 derringer that Ed had later held in his hand.

The slides showed how the markings on test bullets matched those on the partial slug that had killed Beth.

When Leaks had finished with Sandy I stood up and said, "The defense has no questions of this witness."

Once again Steinmetz gave me an approving look when I sat down.

The prosecution's next witness was Ann Jellicoe, who'd attacked me with her screwdriver at the country club on Friday, five days before. It seemed an age ago now.

"I have her on cross-examination," Steinmetz whispered.

I agreed again and then thought about it for a moment. "When you're doing your cross stop every now and then and confer with me even if there isn't anything to confer on," I said in a low voice.

He smiled, understanding. It's worse on a witness if the lawyer she dislikes isn't doing the questioning but seems to be egging it on. I figured Ann Jellicoe might blow up on the stand and I intended to give her every reasonable chance to do so.

She came haughtily into court and I wondered where she got the haughtiness. There's a lot of it misplaced in small towns. She was a fat, squat woman with a bad temper. Her biggest successes in life, as far as I knew, were occasional victories in the Friday night ladies' league and I now believed she miscounted her score to manage that. I watched her carefully as she took the oath. She stole one quick look at me and her mouth thinned.

Leaks led her through her name, address, and relationship to the deceased.

"You knew her all her life?"

"Yes. She was, as I said, my niece. She was a lovely, innocent girl."

Steinmetz rose. "Move to strike the last sentence as unresponsive."

Judge Harner nodded. "It will go out." He leaned out a little and smiled. "Answer only the questions you're asked."

"Oh," she said apologetically. I could see a little red color come into her face. She didn't like being ordered to do anything, but then she nodded to herself, perhaps to regain her composure.

"How well did you know your niece?" Leaks asked.

"Very well. She was a lovely, innocent girl."

Steinmetz bobbed up again. "Once more we move to strike the last sentence of the answer as unresponsive."

"Strike it," the judge said, looking out at his court reporter. He leaned out again, but the smile was gone. "Once again, you'll please answer only the question you're asked."

She nodded shortly, her face now two shades darker, her lips almost at maximum thin.

"Did you visit with Beth Sager?" Leaks asked.

"Frequently."

"What do you mean by 'frequently'? Would that be once a month? Once a week?"

"More often than either. I stopped past her home every other day or so."

"By 'her home' you mean the house on River Road?"

"Yes. The house where Ed killed her."

Steinmetz was on his feet. "Your honor . . ."

"Yes, Mr. Steinmetz," Judge Harner said. "I know. That will go out. The jury is instructed to disregard that portion of the witness's answer concerning the death of Beth Sager." He looked at Herman

Leaks. "Did you interview this witness prior to calling her as a witness, Mr. Leaks?"

"Yes, your honor."

"Would you perhaps like additional time to talk with her and inform her of courtroom procedure?"

"No, I think not." One of Herman's assistants pulled at his sleeve, but Herman said a few short, soft words and the assistant subsided. "I'll try to get right to the point," Leaks added apologetically. "When I interviewed her she was upset about the death of her niece."

"I see," the judge said gently. "Well, let's get right to what she saw and heard." He turned to Ann Jellicoe. "Mrs. Jellicoe, he's going to ask you some questions about things you saw and heard. You may answer only as to things you yourself saw the defendant do or things you heard him say. You may not tell here, for example, anything which you heard from someone else or something you believe. You also won't testify concerning anything your niece said to you unless the court approves your answering prior to that answer."

She nodded, hating him, hating Steinmetz, but me most of all.

"All right, Mr. Leaks. Proceed."

"Did you ever personally witness any fights between your niece and her husband?"

"Several times," she said. "And there were lots of times he threatened her I didn't see, but she told me about."

Steinmetz got up. Judge Harner made a beckoning motion with his hand. "Counsel will approach the bench."

We moved in front of him.

"Put this on the record, Sissy," the judge said. "Either you excuse this witness or I will, Mr. Leaks. I'm already tired of her and she's not been on the stand five minutes. She can't follow simple directions and she seems determined to cause a mistrial." He looked sternly at Steinmetz. "Did you and Robak depose her?"

"No, sir," Steinmetz said, when he saw me shaking my head negatively. "We have only her statement furnished by the prosecutor."

"She saw some things happen the state feels this jury should hear about," Leaks said stubbornly.

"She apparently can't separate those things from nonadmissible evidence," Judge Harner said. "Do you want to excuse her or shall I?"

"If she's excused by the court I want to have the jury sent to the jury room and make some offers to prove," Leaks said.

Harner smiled at him. "You ask her another question that she answers the way she's answered before and I'll declare a mistrial, Herman."

"Nevertheless . . ."

"Make your offer to prove at the close of the trial when the jury's in the jury room," Judge Harner said. I could see he was angry and I kept my face without expression.

"Would you excuse her, please?" Leaks said plaintively. "She thinks this is all a conspiracy anyway. She wouldn't understand if I excused her."

Steinmetz leaned close to me. "Another vote," he whispered.

"I'll excuse her," the judge said. "Back to your seats and let's move things along."

We took our seats again. Ann Jellicoe's eyes followed me. Whatever had taken place at the bench was my fault.

"Mrs. Jellicoe," Judge Harner said harshly, "the court's going to excuse you. You may leave."

"I'm not to testify?" she asked. "Any more?"

"That's correct. You can leave now. We're under a separation of witnesses here so you'll not discuss with anyone else who might be a witness how or to what you testified. You're excused now."

She got up. She shook her head like a bewildered golfer who's just three-putted from five feet. "I've got a lot of other things to say about this case." She pointed at me. "He knows them."

Judge Harner shook his head. "Not any more in this court, Mrs. Jellicoe. *You'll leave it now.*"

For one moment I thought she was going to contest further, but then she got up, lowered her head, and plowed through the silence to the door. I heard her heels down the hall. It seemed to me that everyone in the courtroom, judge, jury, lawyers, and all the rest, suddenly breathed easier.

"The jury will disregard all testimony it heard from Mrs. Jellicoe," Judge Harner ordered. "What I mean to say is that eventually you may consider and decide this case. I want you to do it as if Mrs. Jellicoe hadn't appeared at all as a witness in it." He nodded at Herman. "And now, Mr. Leaks, call your next witness."

The next five witnesses crucified Ed Sager. They were, in order of appearance, a cousin of Beth's who was also a Bington police officer, then a business associate of Ed's with whom Ed and Beth had socialized (he was happily married, pleasantly ugly, and Beth had never made a pass at him), two waitresses, one from the Elks, the other from the Moose, who'd witnessed name-calling, threat-making fights, and a bartender at the country club who'd witnessed dozens of difficulties. They testified variously that Ed had threatened his wife with extinction numerous times, torn her blouse (one time only), cursed her (lots), thrown food on her (three or four times), poured a drink on her (one time again, Ed wasn't a waster of alcoholic beverage). Etc., etc.

We brought out on cross that Beth had done her share of damage to Ed, that Ed usually had been drinking heavily when problems occurred, and that many of the fights were started by Beth.

If we'd wanted to make Ed sound like a peaceful person who'd been pressed into a sudden act of violence when Beth was shot I figured that chance was badly bent. The two of them had had too many public problems in too many places. Herman had done a good job with the witnesses. All of them, with the exception of the Moose waitress, had witnessed problems in the year before Ed's trial.

None of the witnesses, despite our badgering, had the slightest doubt as to Ed's sanity. And none of the witnesses, when I probed them, had ever seen Beth do anything with another man, not touch one, kiss one, or make a suggestive move at one. That puzzled me as I plodded along, but then the answer came to me. She had her home for that, a safe place with pool and patio, soft music, and good wine. I remembered my time with her. I wondered how many men she'd invited to see her in her white bathing nude-suit and how many had scooped her gratefully out of it. Some had at least.

She could afford to be discreet with men in public, to put on an act for the town and her relatives.

At just before four in the afternoon, after a long, distressing day, the prosecution rested. We made our obligatory, quiet motion for a directed verdict, which Harner overruled politely with a headshake and a smile. He then sent the jury on its way with instructions to return in the morning.

"The state's best evidence is that the defendant, angry again at his wife, lay in wait for her after hiding himself in the closet of her hall. He was where he'd been ordered not to be. He killed her when she came into the room," Harner told us when the jury was gone.

We went back to our table.

I looked at Ed. "I'm going to call you as my second witness tomorrow, Ed. My first witness will be Wade Smyth."

"Preacher?" Ed asked.

I nodded.

Steinmetz waited with me until the deputy had taken Ed and begun the return to the jail. Outside, in the hall, the curious waited to watch.

"Why Preacher?" Steinmetz asked. "I saw his name on the witness list but I thought it was padding. Preacher, for all else he is, is also a town joke, a character, and more laughs than anything else."

"He knows Ed well and they're friends. Before this last, final drunk of Ed's they did a lot of drinking together. Preacher went dry some eight or nine months ago and is dry now, best I can tell."

"The jury might believe that once a drunk is always a drunk. And Preacher has a reputation for turning on his friends when he's dry and they're not. He watches the courthouse wall from across the street and calls the law when one of his former buddies passes out. How do we know he won't turn on Ed? Surely you've got other, better witnesses who can testify to Ed's drinking habits."

"Herman didn't depose Preacher, Judge," I said carefully. "I'm pretty sure he knows nothing about his background. To him Preacher's just another of the town drunks. I hope he'll tackle him that way."

Steinmetz thought about it for a time and finally nodded. "It can't hurt much anyway. And you'll be using Preacher first. Even if he hurts he won't hurt that much." He was still dubious. "You sure he's dry?"

"Let us pray."

CHAPTER TEN

Trial Lawyer's Maxim: "Ask no witness a question unless you already know the answer."

I went home and got into a wrestling match with myself about the witnesses listed in Beth's diary. If things went very dark for Ed during his testimony then I planned to keep calling the witnesses who'd been involved with Beth until I believed the sting had faded and the jury had other things to consider.

I'd save Tink and Mayor Ferd for last and see what I needed to do then. I was almost sure I could trade them to the prosecutor for an agreement to submit only voluntary and involuntary manslaughter verdicts to the jury along with the various not-guilty verdicts. At least the most Ed would get would be a term of years, forty at top, much less at bottom.

Jo said, "You're pensive again tonight. After this one I wish you'd try to get yourself into writing wills or representing corporations or something neat like that. Things like Jake does."

I smiled at her. "Things like Jake does don't interest me much, Jo. When they come in to me I usually try to get someone else in the firm to do them."

She nodded. "That I realize. You've sat there through television without hearing it. You haven't heard much I said either. You haven't even asked about your son."

"He's all right, isn't he?" I asked, suddenly anxious.

"Sure. I took him to the doctor's today. He's up two pounds since our last trip and the doctor says he's completely healthy. He said to tell you he'd inherited my liver." She got up. "It's time to go to bed."

"In a bit."

"Well, I'm going."

"Yes," I said, nodding at her.

"That big guy from your firm has been watching the house. The new one. Sam King."

"Watching the house?"

"I saw him out there and went out and asked him what he was doing. He said Judge Steinmetz told him to watch things here until this trial was over. I told him that wasn't necessary, but he was still there when you came home. Didn't you see him?"

I shook my head. I wondered what Steinmetz had heard that had sent him to Sam King. I'd ask tomorrow.

"When will your case go to the jury?"

"Late Friday or, more probably, Monday. It's according to how it goes."

"That's not so long to wait," she said placidly. "When it's done we'll get you back for a time." She reached out and patted my hand. Hers was warm and soft. "I'm going to bed now. Come along soon, Don."

I nodded.

For a time I sat there working on it. There was something. It sat in the back of my mind and walked stealthily and I couldn't see it, but I knew it was there.

I slept in the chair for a bit and then I went to bed. Jo slept silently beside me, her breathing even. In the crib in the corner my son cried out and then went back to sleep. I thought about him for a while. When he was of an age where he'd be about to go to college I'd be eligible for social security, if they still had it. Age didn't bother me much. I wondered if it would bother him. Maybe when he graduated from college he could buy me a cane.

I slept.

My examination of Wade "Preacher" Smyth began poorly. For one thing, after a lifetime of black suits and conservative ties, Preacher, when he'd gone dry and seen the light for the hundredth time, had suddenly burst forth in new colorful clothes. He wore a green suit into the courtroom. He seemed huddled someplace deep inside it. He was small and sixtyish, his face carved mostly out of very large, yellow teeth.

Since I'd known him the now eight- or nine-month period was his longest off alcohol.

When I'd first met him he'd been in real estate and he'd been good at it. He'd been married then to wife number two, a stout teetotaler who suspected his mint breath was not the result of a lifelong addiction to mouthwash. In those early days of our acquaintance he'd smuggled whiskey to the country-club golf course in pickle and Mason jars. I'd not known his background and he'd not talked about it. We'd been Sunday acquaintances. He'd used me and others to give himself a certain believability with wife two. All had crashed and burned when he'd spent too many Sundays with pickle-jar lid at half-mast and wife two had figured out what the other odor was under the mouthwash.

Now, he'd been married three times and was back with wife three, a dowager of heroic proportions, on a trial basis. She had money of her own and was only slightly more alcohol-tolerant than wife two.

I knew Preacher also had been many times in the county jail. His most recent visits there had been as a guest of Sheriff Abe Dorsett. Preacher had also been to the state hospital four times for their sixty-day drying-out and agony school. I figured the prosecution also knew that. It was surface stuff.

Underneath it, in Preacher, there was a proud, shy man with other skills and attributes.

The confrontation between Preacher and the prosecution might be a classic, assuming they didn't know some things about him I'd learned down the years.

"Tell the court and jury your name."

"Wade Smyth," he said, not looking up at me, his voice dry and crackly.

"Speak up so they can hear you."

He nodded. "Wade Smyth," he said, louder.

I extracted from him where he lived, that he was "retired," and who lived with him.

"Do you know Ed Sager?"

"Yes. Very well."

"How do you know him?"

"I've known him for years. We became close friends about four years ago." Preacher smiled. "We spent some time together when and after we were drinking. We spent a lot of time together."

"Did Ed drink a lot when you knew him?"

"Yes. Large amounts."

I saw Herman and one of his deputies whispering and smiling together. I hoped the hook was set.

"Did he drink continuously for days and weeks on end when you knew him?"

"Yes."

"When he was drinking did you ever see him have times when he forgot things?"

"Yes."

"Tell the court and jury about those times."

"He'd forget where his car was, he'd forget where he lived." Preacher smiled without humor. "Sometimes he even forgot my name."

The jury was listening to him now and his voice had grown and become confident.

"Are you an alcoholic, Mr. Smyth?"

"Yes. Right now I'm dry and the Lord has seen fit to allow me to remain that way for eight months, nine days, and two hours continuously. But I'm an alcoholic. I can't take even one drink without taking a bad chance that I'll fall back in the sewer."

"How about Ed Sager there?" I asked, pointing.

Herman Leaks was up. "Objection, your honor. Mr. Smyth, for all his practical experience, which the prosecution intends to probe at length, hasn't been qualified as an expert." Herman looked over at me wolfishly and I tried to look distressed. "May I ask the witness some preliminary questions?"

"All right," the judge said. I sat down and looked over at Stein-metz. His face was impassive, but he fell into a coughing spell for a moment or two.

I wanted Herman to do what he was now doing and would have pushed him much further to make sure he did it.

"You met Ed Sager where, Mr. Smyth?"

"Around town someplace I guess," Preacher said, shrugging. "I don't remember for sure when we first met or where it was."

"You said you and Mr. Sager became close friends four years ago. Where did that take place, if you can remember it?"

"In jail."

"You were incarcerated there and Ed was incarcerated there also?"

"Yes."

"Okay. Mr. Sager's lawyer wanted you to testify about drinking problems. Let's discuss your qualification to do that. Where, for example, did you attend elementary school, if you did attend one?"

"In Indianapolis. High school also."

"Did you graduate from high school in Indianapolis?"

"Yes."

"Did you go on to college?"

"Yes."

Herman paused and looked our way, perhaps now suspecting the trap. I smiled and nodded him on and it was, in truth, too late for him to stop.

"Exactly how much college do you have, Mr. Smyth?"

"I have a doctorate in psychology. I also have written and had published two volumes of a projected three-volume series on the psychology of the alcoholic."

On the bench Judge Harner hid a tiny smile behind his hand.

"You're not telling me the truth," Herman said frantically.

Preacher reached inside his coat pocket. He brought out a sheaf of paper. "Mr. Robak asked me to bring copies of my university records. You can examine them if you want. You'll find they're from Indiana University."

Herman was red-faced and the jury could see it. I savored it for a moment and then got up.

"Would the prosecution be finished with its preliminary questions of Doctor Smyth?" I asked politely.

Herman sat down. "For now," he said heavily.

"I'll ask you once again then, Doctor Smyth, is Ed Sager an alcoholic?"

"He is."

"Is his alcoholism severe or mild?"

"Severe. In my opinion he's suffered brain damage. This is manifested by his inability to remember things, even things of a major or critical nature."

I took the copies of the records from Preacher. I looked them over, although I'd seen them before. The court stenographer, seeing a gap in testimony, clicked off her recorder.

I nodded at her and she turned it back on.

"Your records show you graduated *magna cum laude* from Indiana University?"

"Yes," he said. "That was long ago. The drinking got me after I was out of school. I met Ed Sager in jail like Mr. Leaks said. I've been in jail a lot of times. I've been through the alcohol wards at Hill Hospital for the statutory drying-out time of sixty days four times now." He nodded at the jury. "I'm an alcoholic. The only way for me not to be acutely ill with the disease is not to drink at all."

"Did Ed ever mention his wife to you?"

"Sure, lots of times. I saw her too. She was beautiful."

"Was he ever angry when he talked about her?"

"I can't ever remember seeing Ed angry. His usual condition would be best described as confused. Or drunk."

"Did you ever hear him threaten her?"

"I never heard Ed threaten anyone."

"How much time did you spend with Ed in the days after you got to know him well?"

"Until I went dry I spent whole days with him, maybe seventy to eighty hours a week."

"Did you talk?"

"Sometimes. Usually we just sat. He was more fun and brighter than the usual wall sitter."

"Yet you said he was confused. How did you talk to him when he was confused?"

Preacher smiled. "It's a degree thing. He wasn't always confused or always drunk. Even when he was he was better off than most, brighter, more fun to be around."

"For the jury, define a 'wall sitter.' "

Preacher looked at the jury with alert, aged, lizard eyes. Those eyes had seen all, written it down, put in chapter headings, and watched it turn dusty. "Wall sitters are the drunks you see on the courthouse wall. They pool pennies and use them to split wine bottles."

I nodded and quit.

Back in my seat, I watched the jury. Juror McNear silently applauded me with his eyes. I saw something else interesting. The laid-off factory worker and the young, female teacher seemed to have pulled their chairs close together. Once, when they'd come out of the jury room earlier that day, I'd thought I'd seen them holding hands. Two voting as one?

"Your witness," I said.

Herman got some mileage on cross out of the number of times Preacher had been in jail, what his treatments had been on the alcohol wards, and what he did now, which was nothing.

"I talk a lot," Preacher said simply. "I talk to my friends. I park down by the post office. A lot of people I know or recognize come there. I talk to them. I guess I'm just a natural talker, Mr. Leaks." He smiled and looked over at our table. "And these days, if I see someone drunk in public, I report him. I call the sheriff."

"You mean you turn in your erstwhile friends?" Leaks asked, acting surprised.

"When I'm sober I do."

"What happens when you go back to drinking?"

"I hope not to go back. If I did I guess I'd get turned in."

I asked and received a little break in time from the court.

When it came and the jury was out I asked Steinmetz, "Why did you send Sam King down to watch my house?"

He considered me for a moment. "I talked to Jake and we decided someone ought to be around there when you weren't. I called the chief of police. They said they could run a car through the neighborhood, but couldn't put anyone down there all the time. I told Sam it was just for a few days. He was glad to do it. I'm surprised you found out about it. We weren't going to tell you until the trial was over."

"But why?" I asked.

"A feeling," he said. "I've been in dozens of these things. I've had my share of threats. I've never seen one before where the facts were like this one, which has brought on so many anonymous letters, calls, and the like." He shook his head. "It isn't Ed. It's all these people you've subpoenaed. The towns heard whispers about that. You aren't very popular out there." He made a fist and tapped me lightly on the arm. "Jake and I decided you might very well be what those you've subpoenaed are calling you, a son of a bitch, but you're our son of a bitch."

"Thanks," I said. "That's comforting. Now, come on with me."

He followed me to Herman's table.

"Herman," I said. "On the diary . . ."

Herman and his two bright-eyed deputies waited.

"I'm going to put Ed on next. I'll introduce it through him. I'll stipulate and agree with you that only those pages concerning witnesses called or unfound can be shown to the jury. That means if I don't call a witness nothing in the diary concerning him will be shown to the jury."

Herman nodded, suspecting a trap, his eyes careful. "What do I have to do in return?"

"Nothing yet," I said. "A *quid pro quo* may occur to both of us simultaneously sometime later."

Steinmetz and I left them smiling at their table. When we were ten feet away they were whispering among themselves and I heard Leaks say something I'd never thought to hear him say.

He said, "Robak's not that bad."

One of his deputies shushed him before more harm was done.

Steinmetz was shaking his head when we got back to our table.

"Why'd you do that?" he asked.

"I've got this idea that came to me last night. Maybe not even an idea. A shadow thing, a part of a hunch."

"Religion? You got religion?"

"Not that. I figured out some alternate ways Beth might have been killed. They're all pretty fanciful. But with me sitting on the dynamite diary page by page I can sort of control what Herman wants to let into evidence and what he wants to keep out."

Steinmetz nodded. "He'd kiss anyplace you asked if you'd tear a page or two out of that diary. I'm not kidding when I say he's got to get reelected or go down the good old tube."

CHAPTER ELEVEN

Court's Instruction Number Three: . . . for the introduction of evidence is strictly governed by rules.

I introduced the diary as a whole through Ed Sager himself. That was after we'd explained the diary agreement to Judge Harner, who'd smilingly accepted it.

I put Ed on the stand and led him through his background. The crowded courtroom had grown silent and watchful when I called Ed as a witness and I could feel tension in the air.

"Do you know her handwriting?"

"Yes. I lived with her off and on for a long time. I know it very well."

"So you'd recognize it?"

"Of course."

"I'll hand you what's been marked as defendant's Exhibit A and ask you to tell me if all of it is written in your wife's handwriting."

Ed took it and leafed through it carefully again. "Yes. This was written by Beth."

I offered it. Leaks whispered to his assistants for a time. I thought they were arguing.

"No objection," he said.

I took the diary from him up to the bench and put it in the stack of exhibits there without asking to exhibit it. Herman watched it all the way, his eyes wary.

"You've been here in court all through this trial haven't you, Mr. Sager?"

"Yes."

"Tell the court and jury if your wife, Beth Sager, could have been pregnant by you on the date of her death on March 19 of this year?"

"She couldn't have been."

"Why not?"

"Because the last time I lived with her as husband and wife was late last summer, almost a year ago now. I was not intimate with her after that time."

"Not even once?"

"No. Not once."

"You've seen her though?"

"Yes. Many times."

"Were the meetings friendly?"

Ed shook his head. "They were seldom friendly."

"After you separated last summer how many times do you think you and she saw each other?"

"Perhaps a dozen. Maybe more."

"During those dozen meetings did you ever seriously harm her?"

"No. Sometimes I wanted to hurt her, but I never could. I told her she was a bitch, I called her names. I threw a drink and some food on her. Once, I tore her dress. But I never hurt her."

"All right, Ed. Let's go back to the day your wife died earlier this year. On that day last March did you visit your wife?"

"Yes. I went to the house early in the afternoon. I'd had a few drinks before I drove out there to quiet things inside me."

"Did your wife ask you to come?"

"No. And I know there was a court order that ordered me not to go around the house. But the divorce had been pending since the summer before and I was tired of it. I wanted to know if she was going to divorce me so I went to the house to talk. The waiting time was long up on the divorce."

"What do you mean when you say 'the waiting time was long up on the divorce'?"

"The cooling-off period. She'd filed months before. She could have gone in and gotten her divorce anytime she wanted, but she'd been sitting on her hands. So I went to see her. I told her I might file bankruptcy."

"And what happened when you told her that?"

"She said I'd been drinking. She told me to go walk it off. She wouldn't let me in the house."

"You weren't in the house the first time you went that day?"

"No, sir. She met me at the door. She told me there that she'd probably go through with the divorce and do it soon. I remember that calmed me down some and it also made me feel bad."

"What was Beth's condition when you first talked to her?"

"I don't know. I guess she was okay."

"Had she been drinking?"

"I don't know. She might have been."

"Okay, Ed. What did you do then?"

"I left my car there in the drive. I walked down by the river. It was cool outside, but not real cold. I had a flask. I drank it all, the whole damned thing. I remember a little about going back to the house. I guess maybe I'd been gone about an hour or so, maybe longer. I can remember the door."

"What do you remember about the door?" I asked. He'd never said anything about the door before.

"I thought it was locked and I tried to get my key into the lock, but I guess she'd had the locks changed. My key wouldn't fit. But the door wasn't shut tight." He shook his head, his eyes lost someplace. "I don't know what happened very well from then on. I know I came up and became aware once and I saw her bloody head and my little pea gun there in front of her. I got it off the floor and held it. I got a bottle from her cabinet after I fell into it. I drank some more. Then Sheriff Abe came."

"Do you remember being in a closet in the hall of the home you and Beth owned?"

"I don't remember that."

"How about the other damage in the room. Did you do any of it?"

"Not that I remember. I broke some glasses when I fell against the cabinet."

"Do you remember trying to shoot yourself?"

"No. I remember I wanted to die, but I don't remember trying to shoot myself. I can remember the clicking sounds."

"Do you recall taking some tranquilizer pills you had on you after the sheriff placed you in jail?"

"Yes. I took them all. I had them in one of my pockets and, when they left me alone, I got them out and took them with the evening coffee. But I woke up." He shook his head, maybe still sorry about that.

"Do you recall later taking your bed sheet at the jail and making it into a kind of rope?"

"Objection, your honor," Leaks said softly, breaking the rapport I'd established with Ed. At times I'd stolen glances at the jury. They were listening to Ed raptly.

"On what grounds?" the judge asked.

"I view what the defendant did in jail as a self-serving declaration which has no place in this trial."

"Overruled," Judge Harner said.

"Did you make a rope out of your sheet?"

"Yes," Ed said. "I did that."

"What did you do then?"

"I hung it on a hook in the ceiling. I put it around my neck and swung off my bunk."

"You tried to hang yourself?"

"Yes."

"All right, Ed. Let's get back to that day in March when Beth died or was killed. Did you, on that day, kill your wife, Beth?"

"I don't remember," he said hesitantly. "If I don't remember doing it then my answer must be that I didn't do it."

"Why do you answer that way?"

"I believe that if I'd shot Beth I'd remember it."

I watched his face and quick glances told me the jury was watching it also. It wasn't the best of faces for the situation. The years of overindulgence in alcohol had broken the veins in his nose and under his eyes and taken some of his teeth. His face seemed more facile than sincere, but the voice was good, strong, and sure.

"Now, Ed, you gave the police and sheriff and about anyone else who asked you statements, many of them. You talked to those people time after time and you signed whatever they asked you to sign. Why did you do that?"

"For a long time I thought I'd killed her. I didn't see how it could be anyone except me. And I wanted to die. If a police officer or the sheriff came past my cell I'd think talking to them would help get me more quickly into court and help me die. So I told them whatever I thought they wanted to hear. And I signed whatever they put in front of me."

"Some of the statements differ. Tell the jury the why of that?"

"I just gave each officer what he wanted. If I was asked if I was close when I shot her and angry at her, I'd say 'Yes.' " He nodded to himself. "Whatever they wanted I gave to them." His voice grew softer. "Anything."

I turned to the jury. They were straining to hear him.

"Speak louder," I said.

"If they asked me if I was calm and if I hid and waited for her in that closet I'd say all right to that too. I just gave them back what they asked for."

"But you didn't kill her?"

"No," he said. His eyes left mine and he shook his head. He hedged a little, which I'd thought he'd do, either when I had him or Leaks got to him. "If I did it to her I don't remember anything about it."

"Do you remember anything else that happened that day, anything the jury hasn't heard, anything at all?"

He thought for a moment and then shook his head. "I guess not. I remember the drinking by the river and stumbling back up the hill. When I was climbing back I staggered and fell a time or two. I remember the sound of the river and other sounds." He shook his head once more.

"What were the other sounds you heard?"

He gave me a look full of puzzlement. "Maybe like someone opening a squeaking door. Maybe like that."

"Have you told me or anyone else about this sound before?"

"No. I told you and Judge Steinmetz there was something I remembered, but I'm not sure what I've just told you was it." He shrugged. "It was a door maybe, just a door."

"Are there doors on the other side of the house from where you entered in front?" I asked, knowing there were.

"Yes."

"Could someone have been in the house and exited from a back door and you not seen them as you returned from the river?" I asked, excited a little. Again, it was something brand new.

"I suppose. There are several doors out to the pool. Beth liked for there to be lots of ways out there and to the deck and garden. So we planned it that way when we built the house."

"Do you think what you heard could have been one of those doors?"

"Maybe," he said, not sure.

"Ed, was your wife, Beth, cheating on you?"

I saw Leaks start to get up, but Judge Harner moved a hand in a cut-off gesture like an umpire calling a play. Leaks nodded and sat back down.

"Yes. We fought about that lots down the years. We fought about my drinking. I drank too much and when I drank I wasn't good to her. Maybe it was my fault she ran around."

"Did you ever know about it in advance when she was going to have someone there in the house?"

"Yes. Once I found a note. Once I overheard a phone call."

"Did you try to break in on your wife when you knew?"

"No. I stayed away." He turned his right hand over, looked at the newly revealed surface in surprise, and then held the hand out beseechingly. "I didn't want to catch her, Mr. Robak. I loved her. She had her sickness and I had mine. I thought someday I'd maybe get over mine and she'd get over hers and it would all be right again." He nodded to himself, convinced for now that such was the way it was.

I took a glance over at Herman Leaks. He was in deep conversation with one of his earnest deputies so I slipped in a repeat question. "Once again, Ed. Was your wife, Beth, cheating on you?"

"Yes."

"Did you shoot her?"

"I don't remember doing it. I guess I'd remember it if I'd shot her. I don't remember. So I'm saying I didn't do it."

It sounded lame, even to me.

"What you're saying here today is the truth and there was no truth in what you said in statements made to various law officers in the days after Beth was dead and you wanted to die?"

"Yes. It's the truth."

I nodded at Herman. "Your witness."

Leaks got heavily to his feet. He paced up and down the courtroom. For the next five hours or so, both before and after the lunch break, he deviled Ed with the prior statements he'd made.

"Did you say that then?" he asked, glowering.

"Yes. I sure said it."

"But today you say that it's not true and you want the jury to believe what you're telling them now."

"Yes."

"Then you lied then?"

"I didn't lie. I just went along with what you and your policemen put before me, Herman."

Leaks got red-faced and irritated at hearing his first name used from the stand by a man accused of murder. He bored on.

"When you made those statements it was a lot closer to the time your wife, Beth, was murdered, wasn't it? Closer than now?"

"Yes."

"Then don't you agree that statements made closer to an event tend to be more accurate than those made later?"

"In some cases," Ed said, smiling a little.

"But not in your case?"

"No. I wanted to die when I was first arrested. I hoped if I gave you people exactly what you wanted you'd oblige me."

"We may yet," Leaks said.

I was up. "Move to strike, your honor. If Mr. Leaks wants to testify let him get himself sworn."

"It can go out," the judge said. "Do you want the jury admonished?"

"No. I hope the jury knows enough by now to realize when Mr. Leaks is testifying and when Ed Sager is."

Herman charged back. He got up in Ed's face. "Didn't you lie in wait for your wife in that closet and then kill her when she came home?"

"Came home from where?"

"From wherever."

"She was there when I got there."

"Didn't you plan to kill her?"

"No."

"You threatened her, didn't you?"

"Yes. I'm sorry to say I did."

"And then killed her?"

"No."

"Then who did it? They found you with the gun in your hand. They found no one else, nothing to show another or others had been there. Who killed her?"

Ed leaned forward. I could tell the ordeal was beginning to get to him some, but I held up objecting. He'd have to make his own way and the longer I prolonged it by useless objections the worse it could be. So I sat. Steinmetz looked over once and inclined his head. I thought he was thinking the same thing I was.

Ed said, "I've thought about it some. Maybe the person who killed her was the father of her unborn child."

"And you say that wasn't you?"

"No. We'd been separated for a long time before she got pregnant. She wasn't pregnant by me."

"Are you sure? You drank a lot and your memory of that day isn't so good. Maybe you had other times of forgetfulness before the day Beth was murdered. Couldn't it have happened that way? You were intimate with her and then forgot?"

Ed was silent for a long moment. I'd introduced the sexy pictures of Beth into evidence and one of them lay on the bench at Ed's elbow. He reached over and picked it up and I silently applauded.

He looked at it. "I'd never have forgotten."

Leaks kept after him doggedly. He got Ed to admit he'd been angry on the day of the murder, he got him to say again how much he'd been drinking, and then he dug around in the crevices of the situation where Beth had ordered him to leave and that there'd been no agreement for him to return, at least no spoken one.

But all in all, when he turned Ed loose, I knew it had been Ed's day. I knew they still had him in the noose and that his testimony meant little against the overall evidence the state had adduced, but at least he'd tried. No matter what happened up the line I doubted now that Judge Harner would order a death sentence even if the jury unaccountably recommended one.

Leaks finished with Ed at day's end. Judge Harner sent the jury home for the night with the normal admonition. I waited until they were gone to give Ed an approving look.

"You did well, Ed," Steinmetz said.

Ed nodded meekly. "I did my best." He looked at me, his eyes surprised. "I guess I don't want to die anymore."

A hovering deputy sheriff took him away to return him to the jail.

Leaks came to our counsel table. He stood there watching us.

"I sure appreciate you changing your mind and not parading some sensitive people into this," he said.

"I haven't made up my mind yet, Herman. I'm going to bring them on if I need them. If I don't call them there'll be a reason for it and you'll know it."

"Like what?" he asked, suspicious again.

"Like before I decide I may want to talk to both of them. I won't make up my mind until then. If we run out of witnesses tomorrow then I'll talk to them then. If not, I'll talk to them over the weekend."

"All right," he said. "Okay. But admit I got your man cold on voluntary manslaughter and maybe more than that. You quit now and I'll go for the twenty-year deal."

"I've got my doubts you'll get much more than that out of judge or jury," I said. "So I'm thinking. I might do business below where you're talking."

He shook his head. "Dealing with you two guys is like dealing with a box of snakes." He smiled without warmth at Steinmetz. "You never know where the next bite's coming from."

Steinmetz laughed openly. "Oh to see ourselves as others see us."

"What you're doing is making those poor guys sweat. Isn't that it, Robak?" Leaks said nastily, ignoring Steinmetz.

"Why would I do that?" I asked innocently. "I went to the mayor up front and he wouldn't discuss this case with me. The commissioner brought his .22 when he came to see me about it. No one seems to know the answers to the questions I need answered. Who fathered Beth's baby? Who's George Pitchford? So I want to talk with your two people again before I decide what to finally do, Herman." I patted him gingerly on the back. "Why worry? Election is almost four months off."

"You'll promise to talk to me again before you finally decide?"

"Sure," I said. "And when I say I'll do something then I'll do it. I don't run my business with a backhoe."

Herman turned away, his face downcast. He'd been prosecutor for almost eight years and I could tell from his look he was now envisioning that time having passed. He had nothing else, at least as far as he was concerned. There was a whole, big world out there beyond prosecuting people, but he didn't see it.

When he was gone Steinmetz said, "There goes another reason I put Sam King watching your house."

"Herman?"

He nodded gravely. "Herman. Did you ever see anyone want something bad enough to kill for it? Once again, he has to get reelected, Don."

"I see." I shivered though the room wasn't cold. "Thanks for putting Sam out there."

"Well, it'll all be done in a few days and then things will get back to normal."

"That's what Jo said."

"Where to now?" He picked up his file from the counsel table.

"I want to take another look at something," I said. I dug in my billfold and found the key to the Sager house, which I'd borrowed days ago and not returned. When Ed had said something about a squeaking door it had reminded me I still had it. "I'm going to drive out to the Sager house and look things over once more."

He smacked his lips. "There goes bourbon if you can stand company. This trial has got me so all roiled up my stomach's turning to acid again."

"I'd like to have you go along," I said. I thought for a moment. "If the trial's bothering you that much then you can stop and I'll try it alone."

His face changed subtly and I knew I'd said a very wrong thing out of my concern for him. I went quickly on, correcting things. "Of course if you hadn't been with me we might still have a client with a death wish. You found out Beth was pregnant so you get the credit for Ed's change of heart. I sure hope you can stick it out, stomach acid or not." I smiled. "Try a mint instead of bourbon."

He grinned, appeased.

I really loved the old man. I also knew he was smarter, sharper, and a better lawyer than I'd ever be.

He hefted his file. "I'd not quit now if I was sure tomorrow would finish me off."

I remembered when he'd come off the bench and into the office. "I'm coming in because of you, Robak," he'd confided. "You're always into something. Trouble follows you."

CHAPTER TWELVE

Steinmetz's Law: "If you open a can of worms you shouldn't be surprised when your case is reduced to a crawl."

We took my Ford and drove out the River Road. Along it, in the late Thursday afternoon, the sun beat down hotly on the trees and shimmered upward in reflected waves from the highway. Now and then, through leaves so green they seemed blue, you could see old Muddy, the river. At a bend we heard two towboats hooting solemnly, like owls in chorus at night.

I found the turnoff road and drove up to the Sager house. It was still an imposing sight, but now it was beginning to look abandoned. Someone, vandal or thief, had thrown a rock through one of the windows and a shutter guarding another hung askew, probably having blown that way in the last storm.

Steinmetz and I walked up the brick path. The grass had grown high. The realtor should have done something about it, but I knew big, expensive houses weren't selling now, that the realtor was in financial trouble himself, and he'd taken the property on for the publicity it brought.

The key worked in the lock and we entered. The house seemed the same as when I'd last been inside. If anyone had entered since then there were no overt signs of it. With the air conditioner long off it was very hot inside. Steinmetz took off his hat and wiped his face with a handkerchief.

"Whew," he muttered. "It's got to be a hundred-plus in here. Let's look over what you wanted to look over quick and get back out into the air."

I nodded in agreement. I opened and walked out the double doors and past the pool, full now to tempt buyers. Outside, even in the sun, it was cooler. There were two other house doors leading out to the pool and deck area, one from the three-car garage, and another from what had once been Ed and Beth's bedroom.

Past the pool there was a high brick wall to shield it from wind and view. There were two huge, iron gates through the wall. Those gates led to a garden behind.

Ed would have exited to the river and reentered the house, if his testimony was truthful and if he remembered correctly, through the front door. It opened on to a hall that led to the living-family room, which fronted the pool. In that room Beth had died.

If Ed had heard another door it would have had to be an exit door to the pool or one of the doors that led through the brick wall to the garden.

I conducted a simple experiment. I opened and closed all the house doors leading to the pool while Steinmetz watched curiously. The bedroom door opened and closed soundlessly, but that was no guarantee it had in March. So did the door from the garage to the pool. It slid open and shut without sound. Only the double doors that opened directly to the pool made noise when they were swung. They clicked and squeaked.

I did little good with the two gates. They both made only the tiniest of noises when they were swung open and closed. They were balanced in some cunning fashion so that no matter how they swung they returned to the same position between the brick walls without there being a latch there to catch and hold them.

Steinmetz watched. "What are you thinking about other than the obvious things?"

"Ed said he heard a door."

"That's part of the obvious."

"When he came back someone could have been inside the house, someone waiting and watching. That person could have then gone through a door and outside. I figure it would probably have been the double doors. That person would have wanted to know what was going to happen. Something had been set up. The person would need to know whether and how it would work. But where would he go to see it all from?"

"In March there'd be no bushes in bloom, no leaves, no cover," Steinmetz said. "Tell me why a watcher would wait."

"I thought maybe it would be to come back and kill Ed also if that was necessary. Make it look like murder and suicide?"

"Maybe."

"Let's look around some," I said. "Figure out for me where someone who had to do it would watch."

We tried behind the iron gates, but you couldn't get a good angle on the windows from there and could see only a small portion of the room beyond. The wall between the gates was high enough to block a tall man's view. Inside the wall the trees and bushes were small and formed no cover.

"Maybe he could have waited on one side or the other of the window itself and peeped in," I said.

"Possible, but not probable." Steinmetz looked around the area. "It was March and cool. My best bet would be your someone, if there was one, would be in the empty pool itself."

"The pool?" I asked.

"Of course. A watcher could have seen about everything from the pool, then moved on once he saw what Ed was doing inside, that he'd picked up the murder weapon, that he was drunk and falling around and drinking more, and that he was trying to shoot himself."

"Who would have had that kind of nerve?" I asked.

"You supply the answers. It's your fantasy. Maybe the kind of person who'd have the nerve would be the kind of person who'd chase after Beth." Steinmetz gave me an almost bored look. "What we have to deal with now are cold facts and a trial we're going to lose, not bad, but not good either. I was watching the jury today. That jury doesn't believe what Ed said today except for maybe my old friend, McNear, the Number One Juror. He knows how bad and good Beth was. He kept nodding at everything that went Ed's way. He might hang it for us, but more probably he'll go down with all guns blazing after fighting the good fight and getting the degree of guilt lowered. I figure the rest of the jury will be sympathetic to Ed by the time we get done, but they'll add up the evidence and figure Ed killed Beth. They'll assuage their tiny doubts by going along with

McNear and convicting Ed of some lesser included offense. So long
Ed, but the shape our penal system is in, probably not for long."

"It could have happened the way I'm imagining it," I said.

"Sure. How about a moon-cheese sandwich at the Moose when
we get back to town? They come in nine different shades of green."

I ignored him. "Let's go through one of the gates and on around
to the car."

"Best idea yet," he said. He followed and I led. I could hear him
breathing behind me, his breath heavy and labored in the hot afternoon. It wasn't a good place for me to have brought him. He'd had
heart problems, but I knew he'd not now take kindly to being left
behind, ignored, or not used.

The garden was a ruin. Here and there a few flowers still rose to
the sun, but weeds had taken over most of the once orderly rows. I
remembered when Beth had walked me through them. The garden
had been her one other hobby other than men and puzzle games
and crosswords. A peculiar woman, odd, unusual.

We walked on around the house. I stopped again.

"After he saw what was happening our shadowy pool person went
someplace and called the sheriff," I said, trying that addition on for
size. "Guess for me where he'd go? You know Bington much better
than I."

Steinmetz grinned and considered it. "Probably town. It isn't that
far, a mile or so maybe. There are dozens of telephone booths on the
streets, in parking lots, and in businesses at the edge of town. There
are probably fifty outdoor phone booths on the campus of the university alone."

"So he went to town and he used a phone."

"Even if you're right the trail is very cold. We're stuck in a real-
life situation. Our job's Ed and his trial, not chasing ghosts."

"Do you think the judge would let the jury view the scene of the
crime if we asked for it at this late date?"

He shook his head. "There are pictures of the scene already in
evidence, seasonal pictures, taken at or near the time of Beth's
death. Whatever you need here is already in. The judge seems to be
kind of on our side now. Let's not alienate him by asking for something he'd think cumulative or time-wasting."

"The photos don't show the pool area," I said.

"True, but the pool area isn't involved in what's necessary to complete the trial of Ed Sager. What you need is a miracle. What you'd have to do is get one of those witnesses you've subpoenaed to confess on the stand for the jury." He grinned. "Put on a show for them. Barring something like that, Ed will get convicted."

"If someone else did it then that someone thinks he's safe by now."

Steinmetz nodded. "Is safe," he corrected.

"No. Not until the trial's done." I took another long look at the house, but nothing new came. Ed had said nothing about another car being there. If a shadowy killer had been in the house that someone might have come in Beth's car or some other way. A cab? Once, in another Bington case, I'd tried to check out taxi records and had found that taxi companies weren't required to keep them under our state law.

I wondered if an intoxicated Ed might have missed seeing a car in the garage when he returned and then might also not have heard it slip away?

Or a visitor could have parked and secreted a car down off the highway and walked up? That was possible.

I got back into the car, mind still working. Steinmetz got in on the passenger side. Steinmetz had it figured right. I was a functionary in a play that must proceed by unwritten but known lines. My job was to do what I could for Ed, confuse, object, table-pound, and raise hell. My job was to fight for Ed and get him off with his life and as little time to serve as possible. I'd already done him a job. We'd begun the trial with him wanting to die and the state most anxious to oblige him. Things had changed and now the beginning was clouded and I was about certain I could trade Herman Leaks' two witnesses for a verdict that left out capital punishment.

I shook my head like a tired boxer with more rounds to go. I drove back to town and dropped Steinmetz off at his old stone house on Second Street. Then I parked in front of my house. I didn't see Sam King watching it. Once inside, I could smell soup cooking, but Jo and Joe weren't there.

I went to the front door and looked out anxiously.

I saw Jo pushing Joe's stroller down the other side of the street. Sam King saw me at the door from where he walked behind them. He waved.

I waved back. I sat down in the easy chair in front of the television, but left it off. I thought some more.

In a short while I heard Jo and Joe coming inside. She came to the door of the room where I sat.

"I took him for a little walk. He's starting to watch things. Your partner Sam was with us. He's gone home now." She eyed me and the silent television speculatively. "How was your day?"

"Not bad. Where's Joe now?"

"In his crib." She came on into the room and sat and smiled up at me from my lap. "There's soup and sandwiches for supper."

"That's perfect," I said. "Jo, how well did you know Beth?"

She shrugged. "I knew both of them a little. He came here a few times right after we were married to see you. I saw her around the club. She was a good golfer and bridge player, very competitive."

"Did Ed ever seem crazy to you then?"

"All your friends who are in this seemed crazy to me. They drank too much, they chased too much." She nodded at me fondly. "I saved you from that kind of wasteful life."

I grinned at her. "Gee, thanks." I thought for a moment. "I guess the only semi-sane and sound bachelor friend I've had, since we've been married and outside the legal-eagle field, is Doc Tyne."

"Nope. He's crazy too. I saw his little girl today, the one he had at the club. The one who jiggles." She gave me a severe look. "The one who felt your leg."

"I remember."

"She was in the grocery store when we were in the grocery store. She made over little Joe, but I don't think she really liked him or would like any kid, for that matter. She kept her distance. She said she and Doc Tyne were already kind of broken up. She said he was chasing some married lady." She smiled. "He'll catch her too. He pinches good."

"That makes an opening for me with her if you run off with Doc and leave me."

She wiggled on my lap. "Keep talking and I might do just that.

Doc's new lady is a doctor lady who's fresh-hired at Hill Hospital. I heard about her at golf Wednesday. She's married, but I guess she's about to get her divorce."

"I see," I said. Years back, before Jo, I'd gotten rich off Tyne's discards. One merely waited. He fell in and out of love quickly. He was a better sprinter than marathon man.

Jo watched me. "Tell me what's going on in your case?"

"Tomorrow I'll call Ed's brother and son and a couple of the men who were chasing or being chased by Beth."

"What for?"

"To let the jury see the other side. To show the jury why Ed killed Beth, if he did kill her." I stopped and considered the time situation. "Tomorrow's Friday. What with arguments and all I'd guess we won't finish. I need the weekend to think about the rest of the witnesses and maybe talk to them. Monday I'll decide. Then it's psychiatrists, plus rebuttal. I'd guess it'll go to the jury Monday night."

"Are you going to win or lose?"

"Steinmetz thinks they'll convict Ed. I guess I do too. But it won't be capital murder. I'm betting I can get Herman Leaks to drop that part of it." I patted her. She was firm and pleasantly heavy in my lap. She smelled of soap and soup and Joe and I liked it.

"Soup and a sandwich in two minutes," she said, getting up.

I tried to grab her and was unsuccessful.

In the morning we called Giles Sager first and then Ed Jr. They were sworn and took the witness stand and related horror stories about sweet Beth.

"Ed, how old are you?" I asked.

"I'm seventeen, Mr. Robak."

I watched the jury watch him. He was a handsome boy and the women jurors, young and old, were entranced by him. He came over clear and straight. His hair was short, his clothes neat and clean.

"Did your stepmother ever make a pass at you?"

He blushed. "Yes. Several times."

"What exactly did she do?"

He looked down at the floor silently and I had to prompt him. "Tell the jury what she did, Ed."

"She came into my room. She wasn't wearing many clothes. The first time it was one of those thin nighties. A couple of times she'd be wearing one of her see-through shirts."

"Did she ever try to do anything to or with you?"

"No. She'd stand by my bed and talk and smile. Once she sat on the side of the bed."

"Did she touch you?"

He shook his head.

"By shaking your head do you mean she didn't touch you?"

"She didn't touch me."

"What did you do concerning this? What steps did you take to avoid it?"

"I moved in with my aunt and uncle."

"How long ago?"

"Last fall, early in the fall."

"Did she ever call you and ask you about why you'd moved?"

"No. I thought later that maybe that was what she wanted, me out of the house."

Herman started to get up and then sat back down.

"Why would she want you out of the house, Ed?"

"Well, there were always other people coming and going. I'd go to bed early lots because I had to get up for school and I'm on the swim team. Sometimes I'd wake up and hear her down there by the pool, laughing and talking. I'd hear other voices also."

"Male voices or female voices?"

"Mostly male voices. One time in maybe last August or early September I got up from bed and went down the hall and looked out at the pool because there was so much noise coming from there. She was in the pool and there was a man with her. They weren't wearing any suits." He nodded. "I wasn't sure at first, because she had a white bathing suit she liked and it kind of made her look like she didn't have a suit on when it got wet. She got out of the pool and she didn't have the white suit or anything on."

"Did you recognize the man in the pool?"

"No. I didn't try. I went back to my bedroom and closed the door tight. About then was when I decided to move out to Uncle Giles's place."

"Did your father and stepmother fight and argue when they were living together?"

"Sure," he said, seemingly relieved now that I'd changed the subject. "They fought all the time."

"Did your father ever strike her?"

"Not that I ever saw. They'd call each other names and things like that mostly."

"How did you feel about your father then, Ed?"

The boy looked over at his father. I saw Ed Sr. look down at the floor.

The boy said, "He drank so much there wasn't much time in him for anything else."

On cross Herman got Ed Jr. to admit that some of the parties he'd seen and heard had been bigger parties with more people than just Beth and one man in attendance. He also got him to admit he'd not liked her. I thought the damage was small.

Giles went on the stand. He testified about drinking, about how many years Ed had been hard at it, about the dozens of times he'd seen Ed drunk, and that he'd not, until Ed's arrest, seen him completely sober in years.

Leaks dismissed Giles without extensive cross-examination. Giles came over on the stand the way he appeared in life, strong, slow, and sure. Herman asked a few valueless questions, argued with his deputies about more, and I thought they prevailed.

I called the first of the men in Beth's diary.

Sid Gellheiser was a widower. He owned a great deal of stock in Bington's second-largest bank, was on its board of directors, and dabbled in real estate. He was now pushing hard at sixty. I'd been surprised when I'd first seen his name in the diary, but surprise had faded the more I thought about Sid. I knew Beth had a penchant for youth and Sid was far from youthful, but he fought life to look young. He wore the best toupee in Bington and wore it glossy black, without a touch of gray. He drove a 300Z, ran in marathon races, and did all the tribal dances of the young with gusto. He wore clothes that were thirty or maybe forty years young for him, jeans, T-shirts with pictures on them, leather jackets, and had the effrontery to look pretty good in them. From fifty feet away you could mistake him for forty. Only when you got close did the illusion begin to fade, but even then he looked a young fifty. There was a story floating around town that he'd had a face-lift. I thought it was true.

I knew him a little. He did some of the parties Jo and I did. I'd watched him curiously at those parties. He was a one-drink man. He'd get a Scotch and carry it around with him all night, adding ice. He'd watch other partygoers with sharp, inquisitive eyes, seeing who was ripe, who was discontented.

After the subpoenas had been served he was the only one who'd not contacted me. My bet was he'd probably bragged he was called. He wasn't a man who went into detail on his conquests, but I thought he was pleased the town knew. Steinmetz and I had discussed him and figured he was the best of the bunch to call first.

He came springily into the courtroom wearing a lightly patterned brown suit, mahogany loafers, a bright tie, and his excellent toupee. He took the oath, climbed into the witness chair, and grinned out at me.

"Howdy, Don."

"Howdy, Sid," I answered. I could see Herman Leaks moving restively about.

"Will you please tell the court and jury your full name?"

"Sidney Joseph Gellheiser."

"Where do you live?"

"For the past three years I've occupied the governor's suite at the Bington Broadview Hotel down on the river. I used to live on Main Street before that."

"And what business or profession do you follow?"

"I'm in investments. I also own part of the Broadview. You could say I'm semiretired."

"Are you married?"

He shook his head. "Not now. I was married, but my wife died about five years ago."

"Children?"

"Two sons. They don't live in Bington. One's in Indianapolis and the other in New York."

"Did you know Beth Sager?"

"I did." His voice was strong.

"I'm going to hand you a part of what's been marked as a defense exhibit and which has been admitted into evidence. I'd like you to look it over." I handed him the page from the diary.

He examined it. I saw him frown once. In one area she'd not given him the best of marks and that probably hurt his pride a little, but I wasn't going to embarrass him with it.

"Have you had enough time to look it over?" I asked politely.

"I guess."

"Is that your name?"

"Yes."

"If I told you that page came from a diary that Beth Sager kept could you go along with that?"

"Yes." He frowned down at the page. "There are some dates and check marks that I don't understand."

"Think back, Sid. Do the dates mean anything to you?"

"Some of them could be dates I took Mrs. Sager someplace or spent nights at her house."

"You slept with her, were intimate with her?"

"Yes."

"On the dates listed?"

"I believe so."

"On those days and nights you spent with Mrs. Sager did she ever mention her husband?"

Sid's lip curled a trifle. "To the best of my recollection she never mentioned him."

"Not even once?"

"Not once. I asked her about him a couple of times. She wouldn't say his name. He was always 'the drunk.' "

"So she had no use or love for him?"

"Not that I saw."

"Your page in her book shows you went with her about a year ago, in the summer, for a period of say four or five weeks?"

"Yes."

"Is that the way it was? Is the page you saw correct to the best of your recollection?"

"I'd say it was pretty close."

"Why did it stop?"

"I don't know. She stopped it, I guess."

"Did you see her after that four- or five-week period?"

"I saw her on the streets a few times. I called. She had one of those answering devices on her phone then. She never answered herself. I'd leave a message, but she didn't return the calls."

"Did you ever figure out why?"

"I never did, Don. I was sorry. She was a lovely woman. I suppose she found someone else. I know I did." His last sentence sounded faintly defensive.

"So you stopped seeing her and didn't see her again socially after last summer?"

"Yes."

"Do you have any idea of whom she might have been going with in December or January last?"

"You mean December of last year and January of this year?"

"Yes."

"Yes," he said, surprising me and making my blood run quicker. "I saw her sometime around the first of the year. She told me she was going with a man from outside Bington. She didn't tell me his name. I never saw him. That was peculiar. After she cut me off I used to drive past her house now and then to see if I could spot her. I was still doing that last December and January. I'd park for a minute or two down by the river, but I never saw anything of interest."

"Did you park by her house as late as March?"

"No. I gave it up."

"You weren't intimate with her after last summer?"

"No."

"Did you see her again after the first of this year?"

"No. Early January was the last time. She seemed content—maybe *settled* is a better word."

"Thank you. Your witness, Mr. Leaks."

Herman got up. One of his bright deputies got up with him and they conferred. Herman had introduced me to both of them at one time or another, but the names wouldn't come back to me now. The young deputy whispered at length and finally Herman nodded grudgingly.

"Mr. Gellheiser, how well did you or do you know Ed Sager, Beth's husband?"

"I knew who he was. That's all."

"You've never met him or spoken to him?"

"Not to the best of my recollection."

"That's Ed Sager sitting there next to Mr. Robak," Herman explained. "Are you positive you don't know him?"

Gellheiser smiled over at Ed. "I don't know him, but, like I said, I've seen him around."

Herman asked a few other ineffectual questions and then sat down. He and the deputies conferred with a touch of agitation.

Steinmetz and I managed to hide grins. Small victories are enjoyable when you expect final defeat. Herman should have let Gellheiser go without cross-examination.

CHAPTER THIRTEEN

Ann. Statutes: A person who makes a false statement under oath, knowing such statement to be false, commits perjury, a felony.

I called the next man in the diary and got out his page. He was Stanley Poling, a local used-car dealer. He came bravely in. I went through the preliminaries quickly, name, residence, occupation, who lived with him. He answered each question slowly and carefully. He sat tensely on the witness stand, wearing his lodge pin in his lapel. He was a fortyish man, heavy, but handsome in an overblown fashion. He'd been married, I knew, three times. He wasn't married now.

"Did you know Beth Sager?" I asked politely.

He thought on it. "Vaguely."

"What do you mean by 'vaguely'?"

"I knew who she was is all. I saw her around town some."

"Did you ever visit her house or take her out on dates?"

"Oh, no," he said, as if surprised.

I was getting irritated. I handed him the page from the diary with his name on it. I also took out the pages that I'd copied.

"May I exhibit this page by copies to the jury?" I asked.

Judge Harner looked over at Herman. He nodded heavily. "No objection."

I handed them out to the jurors and alternates. They clutched them and watched the man on the witness stand.

"You have in your hands a page from a previously entered exhibit. Will you look it over?"

He did for a long time. Finally he looked back up.

"Is that your name there?"

"Seems to be," he said hesitantly. He tried to hand the page back to me as if it was poisoned and long touching would lead to sickness and death.

"Another witness just testified in court, after looking at a page like yours, but with his name on it, that the dates listed were dates he'd taken Mrs. Sager out on a date or stayed overnight in her home." I looked down at his page. "There are some dates listed after your name. Are you saying again you didn't know her socially?"

"That's sure the way it was," he said, smiling ingratiatingly. "Maybe I'm an affair she imagined."

I couldn't leave it at that even though I perceived the jury didn't believe him. "You're divorced, aren't you?"

"Yes, but me and my wife are trying to work things out, or were before your subpoena was served. This is embarrassing to me and her both."

"You realize you're under oath?"

"I know that." Poling looked up at Judge Harner. "You know how it is, Judge."

Harner looked coldly down at him. The jury watched the byplay raptly. I saw we had a full courtroom of curious onlookers.

"I don't know how it is, Mr. Poling. You're here under oath and you'll truthfully answer questions asked you or I'll do my best to see to it that you're back in here yourself to answer criminal charges."

Poling caved in a bit. "Well, it never was much. I went out with her and to her house just a few times," he said to the judge.

"Answer the questions Mr. Robak asks you." Judge Harner said testily.

"Okay, okay," Poling said. He moved restlessly on the chair.

"Did you go out with Beth Sager or visit with her in her home?" I asked. "Check the dates for the times."

"I guess so," he said, looking at the page again.

"Thanks," I said, sensing what I'd get from here on in would be more evasionary tactics and wanting to leave him the way he was.

Leaks got up and moved in front of the witness.

"Did you know Ed Sager?" he asked.

I was waiting for it this time. I got to my feet. "Objection, your honor. I asked this witness nothing about Ed Sager on direct and

Mr. Leaks well knows he can't open new subjects on cross-examination."

"Sustained."

"I want to argue that out of the presence of the jury," Leaks said, contentious now.

"That's fine with me," I said agreeably.

Harner admonished the jury and sent them to the jury room. For half an hour Leaks and I argued what was available on cross-examination. Leaks claimed he could call my witnesses back on rebuttal and question them then. I said he could do that, but that he couldn't ask them questions about unopened areas on cross-examination.

Steinmetz and one of Herman's bright deputies argued law and Judge Harner nodded.

Eventually we brought the jury back and the objection remained sustained.

When Poling was released I called Andy Parklin. Once he'd been a deputy prosecutor, but he'd quit. He and Herman were still close.

"Andy . . ." I began.

"Don't call me Andy," he said warningly. "My name here is Mr. Parklin. It'll remain that way to you always, Mr. Robak." He looked out at me from the witness chair, his face dark, his eyes angry.

"Mr. Parklin, then. Did you know Beth Sager?"

"I knew her."

"Did you date her?"

"I did last summer and into the fall."

I handed him his page and again got a ruling I could hand out copies of his page. Each juror and alternate got one.

"Were you with her on the dates she shows on your page?"

"I could have been. In December I was off on my honeymoon with my wife. Before that I can't give you dates."

"A whirlwind romance?" I asked sarcastically.

He waited.

"Beth Sager gave you high marks, Mr. Parklin. Are you sure you didn't see her in December or January?"

"I met my wife in November. We were married in December.

You could have found that out by asking, Mr. Robak. Or by answering my phone calls."

"The evidence has shown that on the date of her death on March 19 of this year that Beth Sager was ten weeks pregnant. Could you have been the father of that child, Mr. Parklin?"

"Absolutely not."

"Do you know anything that you can tell this court and jury about who could have been the father?"

"Not a single thing."

"Did you ever meet a George Pitchford?"

"No."

I picked at him a little more, but without effect. When he was excused he walked back through the courtroom. A pretty girl got up in the back and joined him.

They both turned back to glare at me from the door.

And so went Friday, the last day of the week. When we were done with it I'd shown Beth Sager had boyfriends, that they'd visited her home, and that at least some of them were willing to admit they'd been intimate with her. None of them knew who she was going with in late December or in January and none of them knew George Pitchford.

None of them had dated her or gone to her house after the end of October of the year before.

At the end of the day I was down to Mayor Ferd Hoover and County Commissioner Tinker Clippage as the last uncalled witnesses that I'd originally planned to call for the defense, although there were scores left on my witness list.

I sat there and looked at my list of witnesses and whispered with Steinmetz after the deputy took Ed back to jail.

I did have a nervous prosecutor. He sent his deputies on, but he stayed at his table, fussing with papers, watching us. Eventually he came to our table. He stood there like a small boy, moving from foot to foot.

"This case hasn't worked out as I thought it would," he said to Steinmetz. He nodded at me. "Isn't there some way we can deal it out?"

"I hope so," I said. "I'm just not sure yet, Herman. I would like you to do something for me."

"What's that?" he asked, instantly defensive.

"I want you to give Judge Steinmetz here your home phone number, the unlisted one. We'll promise to tear it up when this case is done. I want to confer with Steinmetz back in the office after I check some things. I want to weigh things against other things, to think about how my client could be helped by witnesses not yet called. Then, if I think we can strike a bargain, I'll call you this weekend. In the meantime tell the mayor and Tink that they aren't off the hook yet, but I'm sure leaning their way. Will you do that?"

"All right. I'll do that. And I'll try to deal. But no wild stuff, Robak. I'm up for reelection this fall."

"I'd heard that," I said carefully.

"I hear the people out there."

I choked a little, but managed to control myself. "Herman, you know we'd not tamper in your political plans," I lied. "How would I ever learn to get along with a new face in your chair? I'm trying to tell you that if anything beneficial occurs to me I want you to be a part of it. I want you to know what it is rather than wander up on it like you did with Preacher Smyth."

He smiled unsurely. "Why is it then, Robak, that I get the feeling when you're close to me that you're after my hat, belt, and overcoat?" He observed me from some far-off place. "I'm glad it isn't you running against me."

Steinmetz laughed. "Robak would never do that, Herman. He couldn't stand respectability."

Jo was playing golf again, it being Friday. I looked at the courthouse tower clock and figured she'd be about halfway through the nine. Steinmetz and I walked back up the street. It was slightly cloudy, but I didn't think it would rain on Jo.

"What are you going to do, Don?"

"I'm not for sure. Something about this thing keeps gnawing inside me. I think we can trade Herman the two witnesses he wants for a dismissal of the major charges. Ed would still get time, but not as much. I wonder if he'd live long in prison?"

"People are tougher than you give them credit for being," he said. He stopped and looked at me. "You've got something more than that, haven't you?"

"Maybe. Something came strongly to me when we were out at Beth's house, but it's farfetched and crazy. Even if it's right I don't know if it would work. But it's something. I want to think on it some more. What I'm hoping to do is panic Herman, get all I can, and then throw this in as a stray bone on the end."

"What is it?"

I shook my head. "It's mixed up yet. Let me mull it over and try to figure out how to use it before I say."

"I'd rather you told me what it was. What happens if you drop dead over the weekend?"

"You know everything I know, or most everything."

He waited.

I relented. "I'd like for you to do two things for me over the weekend. First of all I want you to talk with Mayor Ferd and Tinker. Ask them the same questions we were asking on the stand. See if you can get anything from them we don't know."

"Okay."

"Then Doc Tyne said something the other day about trying hypnotism. Did you say anything to Ed about it?"

"No."

"Nor did I. Do you know anyone in the psychology department at the university?"

"Sure. I know Professor Ryan Short. He's head of the department. He comes to the downtown Moose a lot. In fact, I'd bet he's there now."

"Could you get him or someone he recommends to hypnotize Ed tomorrow or Sunday?"

"Probably. But why do it now? Ed's testified and I doubt the judge would let him testify again, particularly if you start saying the dread word 'hypnosis.'"

"I don't want to recall Ed. And I think we've gotten all out of him he knows. I just want to make sure, just like I want to make sure with the mayor and Tinker. And I want, at some time in the trial, or may want, to be able to say we did hypnotize Ed."

"Why not get Doc Tyne?"

"No. I want someone who isn't on the witness list so that person can't be called."

Steinmetz shook his head. He watched me closely, trying to fathom what I was up to.

"What time do you want me to set this up?" Steinmetz asked. I could see he was unsure about it.

"Over the weekend. I won't be there. I just want you and your Professor Short to see if Ed can recall anything else. My bet is he can't. I want to know if he does."

"With you not there?" he asked suspiciously.

"I'd hate to lie about what happened with me being a witness to the happening," I said.

"I'll see what I can do."

"Don't put any words in Ed's mouth. Again, all I want to know is if Ed remembers anything else. I don't believe he does. And on the two witnesses, Ferd and Tinker, I only want to know if they'd turn the trial around for us if called."

"Why me and not you with them?"

"You're still their friend. I'm not now."

Steinmetz suddenly nodded. "I think I might see where you're headed."

"You know what I know," I said again. "Besides, what I've got is pretty slim and I doubt I can do anything with it."

"I don't see its worth either and I don't believe it."

"Will you go along?"

He shrugged. "Why not?"

We walked the rest of the way back to the office swiftly and silently.

Sam King had left a note for us. It read, "I checked out George Pitchfords in city directories and telephone books for about five hundred miles around. There were only three. One was eighty-six years old and used to live in Mojeff County. He said he was distantly related to Beth Sager and further volunteered she used to visit his farm as a child. The second was twenty-two years old and her name is Georgia, misprinted in the phone book as George. The third was a man in Columbus, Ohio. He's fifty-two years old and lost both legs

in a car accident four years ago. He was interested enough in my call
to ask me if we'd represent him in a lawsuit against the lawyers who
helped in his damage suit. After the above failures I checked out
about three hundred dollars' worth of Pitchfords by long-distance
phone. I found no other Georges and no one else who admitted
knowing anything about Bington."

He'd drawn a small, comic face below, complete with frown.

On Saturday morning I went running. I didn't take my normal
and usual route along the river bicycle path. Instead I ran out along
the river. I stayed off the berm of the highway, running outside the
white line where I could. I faced traffic and was watchful. I found it
was an easy fifteen-minute run to the Sager house. On the way I
counted phone booths. I saw at least a dozen on the campus. As I
came to the Sager house I saw nothing, but I ran on up the drive
and circled the house. I stopped at the first of the iron gates. The
pool inside had a few morning insects and leaves floating in it. I
trotted on along the wall.

Something buzzed along the wall and went away. There was a
distant sound. I thought it might have come from the river and I
couldn't tell exactly what it was. I fell limply and rolled into the
garden. I lay there for a long time watching. No other sound came. I
wasn't sure if I'd been shot at or not, but I suddenly decided it
wouldn't be bright to try to figure it out on the scene. I crawled
through the garden, hugging cover, until I got the wall behind me at
its corner. Keeping the wall behind me, I loped away. I stayed on
the hill and did not move back to the road. I ran faster returning
than I had going out. I reported the possible shot to a dubious
deputy who'd probably been warned about me. He thought, if anything, it was probably a stray hunter's shot.

"What's in season?" I asked.

He promised to investigate. I told him to tell Abe I was counting
on it.

Jo and Joe were up at home. I had a Spartan breakfast of juice,
toast, and black coffee. I said nothing about the shot.

"You seem wide awake and chipper this morning," Jo commented while Joe gurgled happily at me when I gave him a piece of my toast.

I'd showered and was in soft, clean jeans and a favored T-shirt that read "Honest Lawyer Inside" on the front.

Jo watched me suspiciously. "Something's happened, hasn't it? Something's come along to your advantage in the Sager trial?"

"I know nothing," I protested. "We have found that some people don't like me snooping around. I'll admit that I've figured out a way for Ed to have a chance. It isn't a good chance, but it's a chance. I'm convinced Ed didn't do it and that Beth's killer is still walking around out there."

"What makes you believe that? What's happened?"

"Let's just say that I've reached a conclusion that there's someone out there, nervous, wary, and worried. I'm working on a plan to capitalize on that."

"How close is the trial to being done?"

I held up a single finger. "That close."

Sunday I stayed close to the house and called Steinmetz. I waited until afternoon. I was in no hurry.

"Did you talk to Tink and the mayor?"

"You betchem. I'm still trying to figure out why you sent me. It's you they want to talk with."

"That's because they want to be released from having to testify. You could temporize with them on that, but I couldn't. Did either of them know anything, particularly about George Pitchford?"

"You know they didn't." He paused for a moment. "If they had I'd have called."

"Then I presume you got nothing new from either of them?"

"Correct."

"How about the rest of it?"

Steinmetz cleared his throat. "At your order I got hold of Professor Short himself. Ed wasn't too much for it, but he went along once he saw I was adamant. You were right there too. There ain't no more. Ed doesn't remember anything because there's nothing inside for him to remember. I guess you could diagnose him as Bourbon-bombed that day. So maybe he did in Beth and maybe not."

"That's one theory," I said, controlling a rush of excitement. "Give me Herman Leaks's phone number."

He read it to me and I wrote it down.

"You going to call him now?" Steinmetz asked.

"Yep. I'll tell you more in the morning. After I'm done with Herman I also want to call Doc Tyne and have him on hand for the morning."

"Hold on a minute," Steinmetz said. "I thought I had this figured, but maybe I'm wrong. Tell me what you're going to do."

"You never reveal sources and I never reveal plans," I said, enjoying it. "Think on it. I'll see you in the morning."

I hung up and called Herman's number. He must have been next to the phone because he answered before the first ring had completed.

"Herman, this is Robak," I announced. "I've got a bargain I want to offer you."

"One minute before you begin, Robak. The sheriff called and said you claimed someone might have taken a shot at you again." He laughed throatily on the phone. "He went out and didn't find one, damned thing."

"Okay. Maybe I'm getting paranoid. Forget it. I thought something buzzed down the wall beside me when I was at the Sager house. And I heard something I thought might have been a shot." I waited for a moment. "You want to talk deal or not?"

"I'm listening," he said. "I think I've got Ed Sager enough to maybe make the capital thing stick, but I'm listening."

"And I think what I'm offering is what might happen at best for the state," I answered. "What I want you to do is drop the charge to voluntary manslaughter."

"How about straight murder? That carries a sixty max, but I'd promise not to ask for max at sentencing and I wouldn't be upset if the judge knocked it all the way down to twenty." He was silent for a moment. So was I. "Robak," he said, "did you hear me?"

"I heard you," I said sourly. "Okay, we drop to straight murder, but we write an agreed instruction including voluntary and involuntary as includeds. We leave in my insanity verdict."

"Okay."

"I want one more thing."

"Okay only to the instruction and the verdicts. What else do you want?"

"I want to be able to call either a witness out of order or recall one who's already testified. One witness. That witness will be called Monday. Part of the deal is you make no objections to the questions asked and that you sit on your hands while I'm doing my direct."

"What are you trying to do to me, Robak?" Herman asked, completely suspicious now.

"I want you to listen to what this witness says. I want to treat the witness, as we proceed along, and if it becomes necessary, as if he were a hostile witness and I had him on cross-examination. I don't want any objections from you or your people. When I'm done with that witness I'll give you back the subpoena forms for the mayor and Tinker and we'll release them." I thought for a moment. "If I get out of it what I'm hoping to get out of it then you give me the nod. If you agree and help me in this, Herman, I'll give you equal credit in the newspapers."

He was silent for a long moment, silent until I was sure he was going to fling my offer back into my face. And it wouldn't work without his cooperation.

"We're under a gag order," he said doubtfully.

I knew I had him. "Not when trial's done."

"All I have to do is sit there and watch you perform and do nothing? Can I cross-examine your witness?"

"If you want. But all questions you ask must wait until I'm completely done with my direct. Nothing before then."

"This sounds crazy to me, Robak."

"If nothing comes out of it I'm the crazy. However, if something does come out then I tell the newspeople you also suspected it and let me do what I did." I paused for a moment to let him think. "If it goes bad you get no problems. If it goes well you get to share in whatever credit there is. Good stuff, Herman. Reelection kind of stuff."

He laughed a small, hollow laugh. "Are you going to try to prove from the stand, through a witness, that someone else killed Beth Sager?"

"Maybe," I said. "It's according to how it goes. Maybe not."

"I got all those statements from Ed. I got the gun and the bullet. I got him drunk and in the house and maybe the closet. This one was always a cinch, Robak."

"Then just listen, Herman."

"If it goes wrong and you get nothing do I get to sit back and laugh about it? Can I say I let you do it and laugh some about it with the newspeople?"

"Sure you can. You can do that as long as you let me do what I want and live up to the other conditions."

"How about Judge Harner?" he asked, his voice unsure again.

"We'll tell him what's happening. I'll get Steinmetz to talk to him."

Herman's voice became surer. "That'd help. Harner dotes on Steinmetz. If Steinmetz tells him something's okay he'll go for it. You'd think they were going together or something."

"They do get along well," I said noncommittally. They got along because they were two of a kind. Herman didn't because he was one of a kind and no one had classified him yet.

"And you promise not to release Tink or the mayor's name to the newspeople?"

"Not me. They're in what's left of the diary exhibit, but you can ask the judge to seal the file and we won't object. Then there'll be nothing to link Tink or Ferd to Beth Sager. That's the reason I agreed to take each page of the diary separately."

"I know they appreciate it, Robak."

"They owe me nothing. I'm trading them for a long chance for Ed Sager."

"He has no chance and you know it," Leaks said slowly. "But you and Steinmetz have done him a job. You've run a probable death penalty down to a paltry term of years. You ought to make him deed you his interest in the house."

"We're in agreement then?"

"I suppose. Why not?"

"I'm making you responsible for your hired help, Herman. Where do you dig kids like that up? They look like refugees from a game show on preppies."

"Delton graduated *magna cum laude*. Ellison went to Harvard," he answered stiffly. "But I run things. Don't worry about them. I'll tell them what to do."

I wondered how much longer he'd run things if his bright boys ganged up on him or found what was hidden under his rock, but that was his problem.

"See you in the morning," I said. I hung up.

CHAPTER FOURTEEN

Rules: Before testimony can be excluded a proper objection must be made.

On Monday morning, while the jury waited in the jury room, all lawyers conferred with Judge Harner in his chambers.

He was acquiescent enough.

"You mean all I have to do is sit there and not interfere?" he asked, puzzled at the request. "I suppose I can do that, if you gentlemen have agreed that's what I should do." He nodded at Steinmetz, trusting him, not me.

Eventually we went into the courtroom. I gave Ed his instructions when they brought him from the jail.

I gave him a yellow pad. "If it begins to warm up a little and Steinmetz asks you I want you to write something—anything—on a page from this pad. You then tear out the page and hand it to Steinmetz. He'll bring it to me."

"What's going on?" he asked, bewildered. His eyes were puffy and his jowls drooped.

"No time to explain now," I said. "Do it like I'm telling you."

Steinmetz nodded sternly at him. I'd talked with Steinmetz before we'd entered the judge's office. He was temporarily persuaded, although I wasn't sure he believed.

They brought the jury in from the jury room. They came in talking and smiling at each other. They'd had a refreshing weekend away from it and they knew each other now. They didn't subside until they were in their seats.

I called Dr. William Tyne. I'd phoned him over the weekend and told him he'd be first up come Monday. He was ready and waiting in the hall.

He came in and took the witness chair. He was relaxed. He wore a blue suit I'd not seen before. It fit him well. The lady jurors seemed to sigh. He had an effect on all females, no matter what their ages.

"Give the court your name and tell them where you live, Doctor."

He smiled and complied. I led him through his background and education until Herman Leaks, becoming bored, said, "I'll stipulate to Doctor Tyne's qualifications."

"Thank you, Mr. Leaks," I said. "One additional thing for the jury then, Doctor Tyne. You're licensed to practice both medicine and psychiatry in this state?"

"I am."

"Did you treat both the defendant and the deceased in the course of your practice?"

"Yes."

"Do you recall how that began?"

He smiled. "I believe you sent them to me originally."

"When was that?"

"Two or three years back."

"Then you were, late last year and early this year, treating both of them?" I asked.

"Yes. At first it was marriage counseling. One of the asides to that became an attempt to treat Mr. Sager and find the causes for his alcohol problems. I also counseled with Mrs. Sager. She suffered from a mild nervous condition. She also tended to be manic-depressive. She'd gotten worse as her marriage and life deteriorated over the past years."

"Did you see both of them often?"

He opened a file folder he carried. "May I look at my notes?"

"Certainly," I said. I waited patiently while he thumbed through them.

"The last time I saw Ed Sager professionally was in later January of this year. He came to my office and was intoxicated when he arrived. I told him to return when he was sober. My records show I did give him a vitamin shot." He ran a finger down a page in the file. "My records indicate further that the last time I saw Mrs. Sager was a few days before she died. She called me on March 16. She seemed depressed. I remember I went out to her house and we talked for a time. I told her to begin again taking some antidepressants I'd prescribed, but which she'd discontinued taking on her own. I thought she'd be all right. She was a resilient lady."

"Did she talk with you about a divorce?"

He nodded. "She almost always discussed divorce. It was an answer she had available. She'd filed for one several times. I believe there was one pending when she died."

"How did you advise her?"

"About what?"

"A divorce," I said.

He gave me a careful look. "I never advise anyone to obtain a divorce, Mr. Robak. I only try to let them see themselves and their situation as it actually exists and not as they fantasize it. That way they can make logical decisions. I count my successes when I put couples back in touch with both reality and each other. I've had some spectacular successes in that area."

"Did reconciliation seem possible for the Sagers?"

He thought for a moment and then shook his head.

I said politely, "Doctor Tyne, the transcribing equipment won't pick up nods or shakes of head. Could you please answer?"

"I apologize, Mr. Robak," he answered formally. "No, it didn't seem possible in their case."

"The last time you saw Ed Sager was when, again?"

"Late January, this year."

"On that date did you form an opinion as to his sanity?"

"I did."

"What was that opinion?"

"I thought him to be clinically impaired, of unsound mind."

"What brought you to that opinion, Doctor?" I asked. I stole a quick glance at Herman's table. One of his deputies was whispering urgently to him, but Leaks shook his head in stolid negation.

"Ed Sager had been drinking for so long and heavily that he had quite apparent brain damage. When he would refrain from drinking, as he did now and then, he no longer would recover and bounce back. Areas of his brain were dead, areas large enough to cause problems. His speech was slurred, his hand and leg movements uncertain. I'd begun to think, even prior to January, that he'd lost much of his ability to reason clearly and that his judgment was severely impaired. But in January, when I examined him, he was much worse. He made no sense when I talked with him. His insights were flat, there was lack of judgmental capacity. He had recurrent delusions and hallucinations accompanied by impairment of his association of words, thinking, feeling, and acting."

"Was this condition severe, moderate, or light?"

He shrugged. "I'd say he was moderately to severely impaired."

"Was he dangerous to himself or to others?"

"Yes."

"Would another psychiatrist, examining him at the same time, have come to the same conclusion?"

"I believe so."

"The condition he was in then made him dangerous, and particularly dangerous to his wife?"

"Yes. When I mentioned her name he fell into a rage and then, soon, forgot why he was in it."

"What was your reaction then to your feeling that he could be dangerous to himself or others?"

He spread his hands. "Most of us, when crossed, can be dangerous to others, but few of us kill other people. To be truthful, I thought most of Ed's danger was to himself. It was quite cold in January of this year. I didn't know where he was sleeping. I was afraid he might fall asleep in the open and freeze. I thought he might drive a car into a tree or another car. I also thought he could have a stroke because his blood pressure was high when I checked it. I even thought there was some chance he might commit suicide. I thought of those things and probably a dozen other possibilities."

"If you'd made arrangements and committed him to an institution then could or would that have helped him?"

"Perhaps temporarily. It would have dried him out just as he's dried out now. I doubt it would have been of lasting benefit. Many of my colleagues aren't much for baby-sitting the multitudes of alcoholics after they've dried them out. As long as an alcoholic patient can function with enough ability to vaguely fathom the world around him he'll soon be discharged back into that world. Most alcoholics, when released, return very quickly to the habit. If a near relative had come to me and wanted me to sign the papers to commit Ed in January I'd have done it, but he didn't seem dangerous enough for me to do the job myself." He shook his head, his eyes earnest. "Doctors get sued and so they tend not to do things on their own except in times of extreme emergency. Ed Sager wasn't an emergency. He was a continuing case. He'd been drinking and so falling into ruin for years." He looked out at the jury, which was listening intently. "His liver was impaired, his kidneys malfunctioned, he complained of constant headaches. His mind was about gone and he suffered from a painful form of arthritis that was exacerbated by drinking. Still, knowing it would eventually kill him, he drank."

"So he drank and it was the drink that eventually made him become insane?" I asked.

Once again Tyne's eyes came up to mine, somewhat puzzled. These were things that I'd assured him Herman Leaks wouldn't let him answer, speculative questions and answers. He looked over at Herman, perhaps waiting for an objection.

None came.

"He drank. Drinking was a symptom of what was wrong with him. As he continued to drink it also became a cause for what was wrong. But there had always been great tensions in his life that contributed to his condition on the day his wife was shot."

"So, in your opinion he was insane on the nineteenth day of March of this year, that being the day his wife was killed?"

"Yes."

"What clinical name would you use to describe the type of insanity he suffered from?"

He spread his hands. "There are many ways to become insane. I suppose his would best fit under the term of schizophrenia, defective affect, manifested mostly by social cultural maladjustment and lack of judgment and caused by brain damage as the result of years of heavy drinking."

I was standing all the way back at the rail that divided the court area from the spectator area. I stood next to the alternate jurors and

I was silent so they could hear the buzz from the spectators behind them.

"Could that be why Ed forgot parts of Beth's final day and his part in it?"

"In my opinion, yes. Sometimes we tend to block out or black out things we don't want to remember. And Ed's mind isn't like the normal mind. It's obsessed by an overwhelming desire for drink. It's diseased. Parts of it, important, necessary parts, are dead. On the day of Beth's death Ed was operating with enough alcohol in his blood to kill a normal person. So, putting all things together, he forgot what happened."

"That sounds convenient for him."

"Yes, perhaps convenient, but sometimes legitimate for a man in Ed's condition."

"Is it possible there's just nothing there for him to remember?"

He smiled a little. "I'd not know about that."

"Do you think there's any possibility that Ed Sager, on the nineteenth of March last, found his deceased wife in their home after she'd either been shot by someone else or had shot herself and that there just might not be anything for Ed to recall?" I asked specifically.

He looked at me thoughtfully for a long moment while the jury watched. The courtroom had grown still again.

"I guess all I can say is that I have no opinion. I did my work and formed my opinion on the theory Ed had committed the crime. My opinion as to his sanity is based on what I knew about him before, not on what happened the day his wife died."

"All right. Will you try to theorize with me, Doctor Tyne?"

He nodded.

"Ed Sager earlier told this jury that he heard something opening, like a door, when he returned to the house after he'd been ordered away from it. Could his memory of that noise be correct?"

"It's possible," Tyne said. "He might have heard something or he might have fantasized he heard something. You related to me he told many, many stories to the police about what happened that day. From the statements you showed me, the confessions he made to various police officers, and what he said in this trial on the stand, heaven knows exactly what happened that day or what he truly remembers."

"After his wife was dead and he either found her or caused her to be that way, he didn't want her to be dead, did he?"

"No. Her death sent him into a deep depression. The depression was intensified by his arrest and incarceration. For the first time in years he was also deprived of his supply of alcohol."

"When you saw him in jail around the time he was placed there did you prescribe anything for him?"

"Not at first."

"Did you later?"

"Yes. I prescribed a mood elevator. He wasn't allowed any medicine that he might set aside and use to do damage to himself."

"Commit suicide?"

"Yes."

"Tell me, in your opinion, had he recovered from his depression?"

He nodded agreeably. "I learned from you that evidence had been presented in court in this trial by the pathologist who testified as an expert for the state that Beth Sager was ten weeks pregnant at the time of her death. That apparently got through to Ed, angered him, brought him back some. I believe he knew, over the years, she was seeing many other men. I can't say exactly why the discovery she was pregnant accomplished what it did, but each of us is affected differently by what happens around us. In Ed's case I'll theorize that his reaction was because Beth, over the period of their marriage, refused to have his child and had openly said she'd have no children at all. Him finding her pregnant by someone else became the ultimate straw."

"Maybe he knew it the day she was killed?"

"From your telling me of his reaction I'd say he did not."

I could see he had the jury hanging on every word. It was time to move to other, more sensitive areas.

"Tell the jury more of the details concerning Beth Sager's problems, Doctor Tyne."

"In short, she was extremely self-centered and quite narcissistic."

"In laymen's terms what does that mean?"

"Narcissus was a young man in Greek mythology who fell deeply in love with his own reflection. Beth Sager was that way. She spent hours in front of mirrors, in dressing herself, in self-admiration. An extra pound or a wrinkle was a thing of horror to her. As she grew older that brought problems. Even though she was still a beautiful woman she lost faith in herself and so had to prove her allure over and over. While Ed drank his way through his business and deserted her bed, she took lovers."

"Were there a number of lovers?"

"Yes. One wouldn't have been enough. She longed for the perfect lover. She'd chase and capture. Discontent would soon edge in. She'd see the imperfections of the new love. She'd abandon it and begin the search again."

"Would this always be a sexual thing, Doctor Tyne?"

"It wouldn't have to be, but the capture would be far easier with the use of sex. It was, for Beth, the ultimate weapon."

"How old was she?"

"Late thirties. I have it in my chart if you want to know exactly. . . . No?"

"Late thirties is close enough," I said.

"Her periods had become erratic. It's a bad time for any woman, but particularly bad for one in Beth's situation."

"And Ed knew of the men and that made him drink more?"

"It isn't that simple to explain. Ed drank before there were other men. He also put much time into building and expanding his business. That didn't leave enough time to admire and be with Beth in the way she both craved and needed. There were arguments and quarrels. The problem could well have happened if Ed had been a teetotaler."

"And the problems got more difficult for them to cope with as the years passed?"

"Yes, but in her way she still loved Ed and he loved her. I decided early in the time I was counseling them that one reason she sued for divorce so many times and then dropped proceedings was that she somehow couldn't face losing him. As she remembered herself when they were married and carried that image inside her, she also remembered Ed from that earlier time."

I waited.

He said softly, "She took lovers and used them in the spider's nest she'd made of their home. I think she believed that someday Ed would return shiny and new. Of course that wasn't to be. Time and alcohol abuse made that certain."

"Then she allowed someone to get her pregnant, Dr. Tyne. Do you have any inkling as to why she did that?"

He shook his head. "I don't know. She never reported to me that she was pregnant. She did tell me she was in love."

"Did she tell you who she'd fallen in love with?"

"Someone she'd met by chance. Someone from out of town." He thought for a moment. "I've lost the name. An older man, I believe."

"What kind of man would he have been?"

"Attractive, wealthy, but with time to be with her whenever she wanted him."

"But you've forgotten the name?"

He nodded. "I've lost it. You told me and asked me about him after you found a diary with his name in it. I've just lost it for now." He waited expectantly.

"No matter now," I said. "Could that man be the man who killed her?" I asked carefully.

I got a puzzled look and a shrug. "I don't know."

"Isn't it remotely possible that he or another of her past lovers was inside the house that cold day in March when Beth ordered Ed away? Couldn't the lover have shot Beth when she demanded something from him or refused him what he wanted? Or perhaps she might even have threatened suicide and, as they struggled for the gun, the lover-visitor accidentally killed her?"

I took a quick look at the jury. They were puzzled with me.

Tyne smiled. "I'm afraid it's not part of my business to guess on things like that."

I moved a little closer to him. "Bear with me, Doctor Tyne. For now I'm only guessing out loud about things that might have happened. Ed Sager now denies he killed his wife. He doesn't remember the act so he says he didn't do it. Is that possible?"

"Ed's faculties, as I said before, are impaired." Tyne gave me a wintry smile.

"But isn't it a possibility that one or more of Beth's several lovers killed her because of either jealousy of other lovers or because of her demands upon him?"

"I'm afraid I have no opinion."

"Could she have killed herself?"

"I told you about that before, Robak. Beautiful women seldom shoot themselves. They almost never shoot themselves in the face."

"Perhaps accidentally then? Maybe she got the gun out to threaten this new lover?"

A small tic appeared near his right eye. "Such matters should be taken up with the officers who investigated her murder."

"But why not with you, Doctor Tyne? Of all the people who've testified in this trial aren't you the one who knew Beth best?"

"Not in the way you're trying to imply," he said stiffly.

"I'm implying nothing. That an implication was intended is your statement, not mine. But having brought it up, were you involved with her?"

"Certainly not," he said, eyeing me coldly. "She was my patient. That was the extent of my relationship with her."

"But you become offended when I ask you questions about her. Is that correct?"

"No, it's incorrect."

"Wouldn't you then, as a psychiatrist and as her psychiatrist, have known how to deal with the situation if, hypothetically, she'd become infatuated with you?"

"Yes," he admitted, not liking the answer or me.

"It's a situation a young doctor like yourself must deal with many times, isn't it?"

"It happens."

"Wouldn't you also have known how to sustain that infatuation in addition to knowing how to make it disappear?"

"Perhaps. In this case it was a problem for her, but not for me."

"A fascinating problem?" I asked.

"Not fascinating," he said softly. "Tragic is the better word." He watched me, very wary now.

I looked around. Behind the bench Judge Harner was now leaning forward, head held in his hands, watching Tyne. His agreement to go along with the joint request for no interruptions had been kept, but I'd seen him moving about restlessly when I began. Now he was still, silent, and alert.

At the prosecutor's table all discussion seemed also to have stopped, at least for the moment. I found myself being watched by three sets of curious eyes.

"I treated Beth Sager," Tyne said. "I examined and treated Ed Sager. That's my only involvement in this matter."

"Do you recall putting me on to the fact that Beth Sager kept a diary?"

"Yes," he admitted.

"And you know I found it?"

"You told me," he said, smiling again. "Early one morning."

"Did you tell anyone else about that diary either before or after you told me?"

"No."

"Did you ever see or examine that diary?"

He thought for a moment. "Possibly. I may have been shown it by Beth. My advice to her was to destroy it."

"Were you the only one who knew of that diary, Doctor?"

"I don't know. Maybe, maybe not."

"When I found it I had the feeling it had been found before. Did you find it, Doctor?"

"Not me."

"Do you know whether or not Beth Sager mentioned you in her diary?"

"She may have. If so, her mention wouldn't have been truthful. I had no relationship other than a professional one with her."

I nodded at him. "To ease your mind, if it needs it, your name isn't there. Another name is. There's a man she wrote about in her diary, the man who got her highest sexual marks. I'm now going to hand you and the members of the jury his page from Beth's diary. That man was called George Pitchford." I handed out copies to Tyne and to the jury. "Is that name familiar to you, Doctor Tyne?"

"Perhaps. I think she mentioned him and I may even have seen him once. I walked to the house and maybe she had him there. She didn't introduce us and she was very strange that day. My being there seemed to make him nervous and he soon left. A big man in his forties, well dressed, driving a Lincoln or a Cadillac."

"You say you walked to Beth's house that day?"

"Yes. I walk a lot. It was blowing snow and it was cold, but I walked. The man was there. He left in his expensive car soon after I got there."

"Do you think you'd recognize him if you saw him again?" I asked.

"I don't know. I didn't see him for that long and it didn't mean a lot to me."

"I see. Try looking at it the way I'm seeing it just now, Doctor Tyne. You're a very handsome man. You like women. You've been married several times."

"Twice," he said.

"Did you or did you not have an affair with Beth Sager?"

"I did not. It wouldn't have been ethical. I don't enter into that sort of relationship with people I see professionally."

I smiled. If you're going to trap a witness you normally need to be sharper and smarter than he is. I didn't believe for a second that I was sharper and smarter than Tyne, but there are other ways. *You can know something he doesn't know.* I now felt cold and sure.

"Do you remember the night you first told me that you'd had no affair with Beth, Doctor Tyne?"

"Yes."

"You brought a date that night, didn't you?"

"Yes. We had dinner with you and your lovely wife."

"What would your answer be if I said your date told me things that night about her marital situation?"

"Probably no answer. The lady was divorced. You know that. And her situation and Beth's are entirely different."

"What would your answer be if I told you your date said that night that the day she got her divorce, after both she and her husband had counseled with you to try to save their failing marriage, that she took you *back* to bed?"

"I'd say she was wrong." A tiny drop of sweat ran down his forehead. He brushed it away with minor irritation.

"That same date later passed the word that now you're dating another married lady. Are you?"

"I might be. Different situations call for different personal responses."

"What's that mean?" I asked.

"In this case it means I told you the absolute truth about my relationship with Beth Sager."

"You knew her well, didn't you?"

"Only as a patient."

"Why are you so insistent on that?"

"Because it's true."

"And it's all right for you to take one patient to bed and not take another?" I asked, smiling.

"I'm not admitting I did do that."

I changed directions. "Was Beth Sager a person who liked to do puzzles and games, that sort of thing?"

"Yes, and I tried to encourage her interest. It helped her some, I think."

"I found some puzzle books, crosswords and anagrams mostly, near where I found the diary. Once more, Doctor Tyne, did you know the spot she hid that diary?"

"No. I told you it might be in her bedroom. She'd want it close."

"You told me Beth visited your office three days before she died and also you've said you walked out there to her house. What did you do on the day she died, Doctor Tyne? Did you see her that day?"

"No."

"There was one sheet torn from that diary wasn't there?"

"There were no sheets torn out," he said positively.

I was silent for a long moment, letting the jury hear the answer echo.

"I'm going to ask the court reporter to read back that answer again."

"He said, 'There were no sheets torn out,'" she said, after the judge had nodded to her.

Tyne looked around the courtroom. He saw me smiling and many eyes upon him.

"I mean of course if there'd been a sheet torn out you'd have told me," he added, somewhat too late.

"Then you didn't tear a sheet with your name on it out of the diary?"

"Of course not. My name couldn't have been in her diary."

I stepped far back by the rail again. The jury was wide awake and hovering on every word. The courtroom spectators sat quietly.

I went back to the attack.

"You told her not to put your name in her diary, did you not?"

"No," he said, shaking his head. For the first time he turned from me and looked up at the judge. "I'm not on trial here," he protested carefully.

"Tell the court and jury what you did tell her about the diary," I said when Judge Harner looked away.

"I've told them. I told her to destroy it. It was something she didn't need, something to be put behind her like little-girl dreams. It was scorekeeping of the very worst and sickest kind."

"I submit to you that you did see that book more than once and that you knew your name wasn't in it."

He smiled, gaining confidence. I'd shaken him, but not much more. "You're right when you say my name wasn't in her book."

"Ah, but wasn't it?"

"No."

"How about a make-believe name, a made-up name? How about a word game, a new name made from your name, a name she could relate back to you, but which you wouldn't know?" I nodded solemnly. "George Pitchford?"

"William Lee Tyne's my name. It's the only one I have."

"Pitchford as in pitchfork. A tine is a spike or a prong, like pitchforks have. There's another, older meaning. It also means, in the same way your name is spelled, to be destroyed or die or perish. Perhaps she had a premonition?"

"Pitchforks and tines," he said, not looking at me, seemingly puzzled a little.

Someone on the jury made a tiny, murmuring sound. I didn't look, but waited until all sound had stopped.

"Would you know Professor Ryan Short, who heads the psychology department at the university?"

The words were a cue I'd given Steinmetz. He turned to Ed Sager and whispered. Ed nodded and took the yellow pad I'd placed close to him. Slowly he began to scribble on it. Tyne watched him. He was sweating more now. The jury watched Tyne and Ed and Steinmetz.

"I know who he is. I took classes from him when I was an undergraduate at the university."

"Would he, in your expert opinion, be competent to hypnotize Ed Sager?"

"I wouldn't know. Perhaps. It's according to many factors." The tic near his eye had become more pronounced. I hoped the jury saw it.

"Have you seen him hypnotize subjects before?"

"I don't recall."

"Come now, Doctor Tyne. You've stated you took a class or classes from Dr. Short during your undergraduate days at the university?"

"He isn't now and wasn't then a doctor. He's a professor of psychology."

"Doesn't he hold a doctorate in it?"

"I don't know his qualifications."

For the first time I put real menace into my voice. "You soon will, Doctor Tyne. I'll ask again whether you have any opinion as to whether or not this professor-doctor could hypnotize a subject like, say, Ed Sager?"

Dr. Tyne leaned forward. His voice was earnest. "I offered to do that with your poor Ed Sager. You refused to allow it and told me evidence obtained under hypnosis was difficult to use successfully in court."

"Correct. That isn't my question for you. My question, which I continue to want you to answer, is whether or not Professor Short has the ability to hypnotize someone like Ed Sager. Have you an opinion?"

"Theoretically I'll say he could. Not having witnessed him in the process, I can't testify as to his success."

"Perhaps it would satisfy you if I called Judge Steinmetz to the stand while you stood aside for a moment? He can testify such a procedure did take place with Ed Sager as the subject. Would that satisfy you?"

Tyne took a quick look at Steinmetz. At the same time he did it Ed Sager completed his scribbling and handed the resulting yellow sheet to Steinmetz, tearing it off from the pad with a flourish. Steinmetz looked at the note he'd been given, scanning it. Like an old wolf, he then nodded at Tyne.

I walked over and took the yellow paper from Steinmetz. I held it in my hands and read it. I stole a look over the top of it at the jury. They sat nervously. Juror McNear was thumping his hand softly against the arm of his chair, like a slow, soft pulse beat.

"Information obtained by hypnosis is not of value," Tyne said, his voice cracking.

I walked back to my former place by the rail. I could see the prosecution table from there.

Herman Leaks nodded at me.

I almost did a double take, but I recovered in time.

Leaks continued to nod at me until he was certain I'd seen it. He sat smiling in his chair. For the first time since the trial had begun he seemed relaxed.

I knew it wasn't enough. Not yet.

"Again, Doctor Tyne, I'll ask you if you were at the Sager house the day Beth died?"

"I've already said I wasn't."

"Would you change that answer if I told you Ed remembers little of value but that? What would you say to the court and jury if Ed did remember you being there?" I held the note out.

"It would be a lie."

"What if I said he saw you crouched down in the empty swimming pool?"

"That's not true," he said. His eyes rolled in panic and he started to get to his feet. I moved quickly and purposely toward him. When we'd been night-running friends I'd usually made his decisions. Now I was making a brand-new one. He sank bonelessly back into the witness chair.

"You wanted to hypnotize Ed Sager because you needed desperately to know what was there."

"I only wanted to do what was best," he said. "I didn't and don't want Ed punished in any way he shouldn't be punished. Look at him. He's better off now." A tiny tear came at the corner of each eye and he wiped them away. "Why are you doing this to me, Don?"

"Isn't what I'm saying the truth?"

"Ed's the one accused of murder. I'm not the one," he answered carefully. He twisted in the witness chair. "You set all this up, Don. I was always afraid of you."

"Yes?" I prompted.

He shook his head and looked away from me.

"Tell the jury what it was I set up?"

"This attempt to hurt and throw suspicion on me."

"Is that what I'm doing?"

"Yes, it is. It won't work."

"Tell the jury exactly what I've said or implied that isn't true."

"All of it." He shook his head and looked away and out the window, closing us all out, court, jury, me.

I waited a long moment.

"Didn't you call me on the phone and threaten me, Doctor Tyne? Didn't you stuff your handkerchief over the mouthpiece? Wasn't that the same way you reported it to the sheriff the day Beth died?"

"No."

"You walked out there and then walked back to make your call?" He shook his head. "I didn't."

"Tell the jury you killed her. Tell them what they already know."

He shook his head again. "I didn't kill her. I couldn't ever kill anyone. I made her love me to save her after Ed began to murder her years ago. He's the one who killed her with his drinking and it all finished last March. That was just the end, not the beginning."

"But you pulled the trigger?"

"I didn't do that. We quarreled and she tried to shoot me. We fought for her little gun. She'd threatened suicide. Several times she had begged me to get her quantities of sleeping pills, but I was afraid to do it. She'd have used them and there'd have been a note someplace telling the world who'd supplied them. She was vicious. She'd been drinking that day. She was the kind who should never drink. It made her hyper. I offered to abort her, but she said she was going to have my child and name me as its father on the birth certificate. She said she'd get her divorce and I'd better marry her. She made threats about the medical society and what she'd say to them. I told her I wasn't ever going to marry her or anyone. I've had two wives and both times it's been disastrous." He looked up at me. "You know how she was, Don?"

"I know," I admitted. "Tell the jury."

"I kept telling her there'd be no marriage and I wasn't going to move in. She brought out the gun then. She said she'd kill both of us. She pointed the gun at me. She pulled the trigger once and the gun didn't fire. I got hold of it and tried to take it away. It went off and she was dead. That quick. It was an accident. I swear it. I stood there looking at her for a time. I wiped the gun and put it in her hand and then on the floor. Then I went to the front door because I was scared. I wanted to get away. I saw Ed coming. I ran out the double doors and hid in the empty pool. I waited to see what would happen. Ed came into the room. I don't know how he ever saw me. I thought I was very careful. Maybe it was in a mirror. I don't know." He looked down at the worn, old carpet on the courtroom floor. "He tried to shoot himself when he saw her. He used the gun. I heard him and saw him. Just like she'd killed herself. The gun."

"Right between the eyes?" I asked caustically. "You shot Beth squarely between the eyes accidentally in trying to take the gun from her?"

He nodded. He lowered his eyes.

I took the yellow paper to the witness chair and handed it to him.

"Read the paper Ed wrote," I ordered. It was cruel, but I needed to do it for many reasons, for Ed, for Beth, and mostly for me. I caught Steinmetz nodding at me, perhaps in approval.

Tyne took the note from me with hands that trembled. He read it. He took enough time to read it several times. When he was done he gave me a nod. His eyes closed tight and he sat trembling in the witness chair. I thought for a moment he might be about to have some kind of attack. Then he crumpled the yellow paper and threw it on the courtroom floor. I picked it up and pulled it carefully flat. I put it back on the counsel table between Steinmetz and Ed Sager.

I saw a couple of men I knew to be reporters get up and tiptoe quietly out the back door of the courtroom. The judge let them go without comment, despite the fact that one of his strictest rules was that no one left except at breaks.

CHAPTER FIFTEEN

Steinmetz's Law: "*Somebody got to win, somebody got to lose.*"

I asked Ed Sager and Judge Steinmetz and even Herman Leaks to join me at the country club. I invited Judge Harner, but he looked at me coolly for a time and then shook his head.

"I guess maybe I'd hire you today, Robak, but nothing more than that."

Herman declined also. He liked me all right, but we don't socialize, you see.

I called Jo to tell her to meet us at the club and that it might be a little time before we escaped and made it.

Eventually we did get there. We escaped the noise, the congratulations, the questions of the newspeople. One of the metropolitan reporters kept calling me Harry or Perry or somesuch. I posed politely for pictures with Herman. He was very much on top of things. I'd saved his elected butt or he thought I had. I let him take all the credit he desired.

At the club I bought round one. I thought Ed Sager, after his long, enforced layoff, would be anxious for a taste of alcohol, but he ordered a lemonade. He sipped it cautiously. I shrugged and silently wished him the best. If alcohol was to continue as a problem there was little I could do. One missed drink didn't mean to me he'd quit. But it was promising.

It was midafternoon Monday. We had the place largely to ourselves. We sat in the big room away from the bar. It was quiet there. Outside, golfers played their intent games out on the ninth green. We watched from a convenient window. I saw Ann Jellicoe finish. In a while she'd come up from the ladies' room and order her first screwdriver of the afternoon, perhaps, not counting lunch. I wondered what she'd do when she saw Ed there. And me. Maybe a four iron?

I tried calling Giles Sager and Ed Jr., but there was no answer. I thought they might be out in the fields.

Steinmetz asked, "I saw how you got to Tyne, but how were you certain?"

"I had a little more information. In his testimony he knew she was ten weeks pregnant. Did we tell him that the day we had lunch with him?"

He shook his head, not remembering.

"He thought we had more than we had and it caved him in. When Doc and I did our chasing together I was almost always the one in charge. When I had him in the courtroom, I did what I used to do back then—I took command of his life."

"How'd it feel?" he asked, giving me an odd look.

"Not too good, not too bad. It was something that needed to be done." I remembered something. "Herman wants the yellow note. I'll give it to him tomorrow."

"Okay, so you knew Doc Tyne real well, but that still doesn't give me enough to figure out why and how you were so sure it was him, to go after him—excluding two others who sure looked better to me."

"It was his girlfriend who first got to me. Doc made me a pretty speech about not messing with clients and patients. I think if he'd admitted taking Beth to bed I'd not have thought much about it or him. But he lied. I got to wondering why he lied. So it started me, while the trial was going on, into continuing asking questions and looking for other answers than Ed here. I think Tyne was watching. I never saw him, but the calls I got didn't seem to be all from people I'd subpoenaed. There were calls about keeping my nose out of things and just generally not messing around, threatening calls, meant probably to keep me closer to home." I lifted my glass to Steinmetz. "You relieved some of my worries when you got Sam to watch my house. I could start exploring things again." I thought about mentioning the possible shot that might have been taken at me over the weekend when I'd made my run to the Sager place. I decided against it. I looked around the table. "Where's Sam?"

"He'll come when the office closes. So will Jake. You keep going."

I nodded. "Doc Tyne's name kept coming up. First off he was our salvation. Then we went to meet him and he came walking to our lunch meeting. Doc's a walker. That makes him different from most people these days. And no one ever saw another car, not Ed, not Beth's callers. You and I went to the Sager house and found us a squeaking, noisy door where Ed could have heard it." I patted Steinmetz's shoulder gingerly. "You were the bright one. First you brought Ed here back to the world of the living when you discovered in court that Beth was pregnant. Then you figured out the only reasonable place a killer could have hidden and watched—the empty pool. I thought some more. Suddenly the fact that Ed might not have killed her didn't seem so farfetched. If he didn't do it then someone else did. So I built an illusion and it worked. Doc Tyne didn't know it was an illusion. He saw me describing what had actually happened. He couldn't get anyone, judge or prosecutor, to save him. So he ran for cover. He went to the story he'd have gone to if someone had caught him in the act."

"Is there more?"

"Not a lot. I guessed he'd lied about his relationship with Beth. I guessed he'd walked out there and back. I guessed the only man she could be close to was Doc. The timing was right. But I knew I could have been wrong."

"What would you have done then?"

"Pursued the mayor and the commissioner," I admitted.

"But we had an agreement," he said.

"And we were able to keep it," I said. "I would have kept it in the trial also, but not afterward. If Ed got convicted he could have used them up the line in appellate proceedings, in post-conviction relief hearings."

"I don't think I'd have done that," Ed said.

"Once you got to prison and the boys in the writ room heard your story you would have," I said, smiling. "It would be instinctive, just like your trying to drown yourself in alcohol after finding Beth."

Ed nodded somberly. "It seems like it happened a long time ago now."

I nodded at him. I kept talking compulsively. "Anyway, it

worked. Maybe it was because Doc advertised himself to me as something he'd never been before, and never would be. I thought if Beth tried for him she'd have been able to get the job done. He's handsome, he was around, ergo, she had to want him. So she got him. When he didn't act like the others that must have made her want him more. So Beth let herself get pregnant. It was a child she didn't want, but she was probably sure he'd not want it more." I stopped and thought. "I suppose I'm sorry for Tyne. Maybe it did happen the way he said, but it's his problem now."

"What will happen to him?" Ed asked.

"Criminally? I don't know. Herman Leaks was tearing his mustache and his deputy's hair out answering that when I left the courthouse. They took Tyne over to the sheriff's office. Herman will have more seizures tomorrow when we present him with the yellow note. All they've got now is what Tyne said on the stand when he was sure I had him. It was enough to get a dismissal for Ed, but not enough to try for a murder conviction on Tyne, at least in my opinion. Manslaughter, maybe." I thought about it and finally smiled. "It's election year. My bet is Herman will give it a lot of buildup and present it to a grand jury. Then we'll see what really will happen *after* election." I smiled at Steinmetz. "Did I tell you we're both supposed to go to Herman's office tomorrow and pose with him for some pictures, all with the yellow note? Herman needs to have the world know this was a joint effort and he suspected Doc Tyne all along."

Steinmetz took a long drink. "You saved him. He's been busily buying votes for years. Other than that he's not too bad. I've seen worse. He may even start liking you after this. You know he'd have given anything for what you gave him."

"Sure, but that wasn't the purpose of it."

Jo watched us curiously. The winning had affected her as much as it had me. She was on a kind of natural high and into her second Tom Collins. Tomorrow she'd be back to normal. I hoped I would also.

"Going to Herman's office and posing with him is something we owe him," I said.

"Why did Doc Tyne take her to bed originally?" she asked. "And why, with his knowledge, did he let things go far enough and her get desperate enough to get herself pregnant?"

"I'll always wonder about it," I said. "I think maybe he figured he could cure her other problems when she fell under his spell. He encouraged her and it got too late, but Tyne himself is as inconstant as Beth had been." I shook my head, not knowing for certain. Mine was one explanation, but perhaps not the final one.

"How about the nest in the closet with the coats down and the wine bottle someone had apparently hidden?"

"I'm not sure whether Doc set it up or it was just like that when the sheriff opened it. It never seemed important to me. I didn't think Ed here would be hidden in it swigging cheap wine when there was better stuff around the corner. But it was another little thing that brought Ed close to the death penalty."

Ed shivered. "I don't remember for sure. Maybe I was in there weeks or months before. I think I got into the house a few times when no one was there. October? November? February? I just don't know."

Jo nodded at Ed. At the same time I saw the front door of the club open. Ann Jellicoe entered. She came into the room where we were seated, perhaps to check the noise. She saw us and quickly retreated.

"Two to one she calls the law," Jo said. "Before they get here will you please satisfy my curiosity, Ed? Judge Steinmetz and Don have mentioned a yellow pad. What did you write on it?"

"Don told me to write something if things got hot. It was hot outside when they brought me over. Then Judge Steinmetz prompted me. I wrote what came naturally. I wrote, 'The sun's hot on my back. Someone needs to fix the air-conditioning in this damned place.' " He looked at me. "Weren't those the words?"

"Accurate enough," I said.

About the Author

Joe L. Hensley has written for many magazines, in both the science fiction and mystery fields. He is the author of nine novels for the Crime Club, including *Outcasts* and *Minor Murders,* as well as one collection of short stories entitled *Final Doors.* Judge Hensley lives in Madison, Indiana.